Fool With My Heart

A Southland Romance

By Meda White

Fool With My Heart

Editor: Andrea Grimm Dickinson
Cover Artist: Kari Ayasha, Cover to Cover Designs

ISBN: 1941287123
ISBN-13: 978-1-941287-12-5

DEDICATION

In loving memory of Jill Cook, a.k.a. Little Bit,
and Phil Hines, my first crush and favorite farmer.
You touched many hearts in your short time here.

ACKNOWLEDGMENTS

Thanks to Mike Bowen for getting a little mud on the tires and to Mr. Hayes for pulling us out of ditches.

Chapter One

Lacy Goodwin crossed her fingers, hoping her old beat-up Pinto wouldn't die as it sputtered down a county road in the middle-of-nowhere Georgia. She thought she was from the sticks, but this was scary.

The property she was looking for supposedly had a big sign, so she couldn't miss it. It was also reportedly only five miles outside the little town of Willow Creek. Her odometer had broken around a hundred and seventy thousand miles, so she had no idea how far she'd driven. If banjos started playing, she'd turn around and haul ass back to North Carolina.

Ahead, a white railing caught her attention. She glanced at the printed email with the directions. Wasn't there something about a white fence? She engaged the clutch and downshifted as she slowed.

Mrs. Baker hadn't exaggerated about the sign. The letters over the entrance to Southland were probably taller than Lacy.

Turning in, she proceeded through the open gate and wound through dense woods. Hopefully, there would be a house at the end of the dirt lane. Her stomach knotted in anticipation.

If she could land this job, it would be the answer to her prayers. It might even increase her life expectancy. She needed to remember to use good grammar, so she wouldn't sound like an uneducated hick. Too bad she didn't practice more often.

Her cotton dress clung to her back because September in the South could still be hotter than hell. Not to mention the humidity. She didn't hold out much hope for her hair with her car's two by sixty air conditioning—two windows rolled down traveling at sixty miles per hour. Tendrils whipped wildly around her face, after slipping from the yellow scrunchie she'd chosen to match her dress.

When the house came into view, she took her foot off the accelerator. Her chin dropped nearly to her chest before she forced it shut. She hadn't expected the house she was applying to take care of to be so dang big.

Huge glass doors and windows looked out from the front of the log and stone structure. It was as big as the motel back home near Murphy.

Just when her lack of confidence convinced her to turn Bessie around and get the hell out of there, Bessie choked and lurched to a stop, a good forty feet from the front door.

"Crap." Lacy stood on the clutch and turned the key over, only to hear the telltale sound of

Bessie laughing in her face.

"Stupid car." She smacked the wheel with the palms of her hands.

She'd *have* to go to the house now. Resting her head on the steering wheel, she let out a sigh. As long as she was here, she might as well do the interview.

Distant memories made her shiver, even in the heat of an Indian summer, but they also reminded her why she had come all this way.

Snap out of it. It's only a job. It's not life and death. With a humorless laugh, she grabbed her purse and a copy of her résumé, even though she'd already emailed it. Thank the Lord for the library and their ancient donated computers.

The car door squawked in protest after Lacy put her shoulder into it, nudging it open. Once outside, Lacy peeled her dress from the back of her legs and fanned her skirt. Judging by the reflection in the rear window, her hair was a hot mess, so she removed the scrunchie, smoothed the fly-aways, and put it up again.

She patted the faded red metal. "Oh, Bessie, why do you hate me?"

She'd have to deal with the car later. First, she had to see a lady about a job, and she hoped like the dickens she hadn't bitten off more than she could chew.

***

Johnny Baker walked in the back door of the main house at Southland just as the front doorbell rang. He went straight into the kitchen and stuck his head in the fridge, cooling off while he reached for the pitcher of sweet tea.

The chime rang again.

"Mama D, where are you?" He poured the nectar of the gods into a cup of crushed ice.

When no one responded, he set the pitcher and glass down on the counter and went to answer the bell. Through the glass, he could see a girl.

It wasn't the right time of year for Girl Scout cookies, so he wondered who'd gotten lost. As Johnny flung open the door, the young lady turned to face him and flashed a big smile. She was a full grown woman and a pretty one.

"Well, you're a slight little thing, aren't you?" He grinned, propping one hand on the door frame.

Her smile faltered a second before she fixed it in place. "I have an appointment with Mrs. Dixie Baker. I'm Lacy Goodwin." She extended her hand.

Johnny took her hand and marveled at how small it was in his own. He could crush it with one hard squeeze.

"Come on in, Miss Lacy Goodwin." He lightly pulled her arm.

She started to take a step forward, then paused and stepped back, withdrawing her hand. After tugging up the scooped neckline of her dress, she gripped her pocketbook strap with both hands, crinkling the paper in her grasp. "Is Mrs. Baker home?"

Tilting his head to the side, he crossed his arms over his chest. "You're not afraid of me, are you?"

"No." She raised her chin. "But I'm not stupid either. If this is some kind of… Just forget it." She turned and stomped back toward her car.

He wondered why she'd parked it so far from the house. "Hold your horses," he shouted. "Mama D's around here somewhere. Don't leave. I'll go find her."

Johnny left the door standing wide open as he walked through the main level of the house calling for his mom. Actually, she was his step-mom, but she'd adopted him and his brothers when his dad had married her. He'd been young when his real mother passed away, and Mama D had been his mama most of his life.

"I'm in here, Johnny."

He followed the sound of her voice to the laundry room, where the washer and dryer were both running. She was folding clothes and listening to the radio. No wonder she hadn't heard the door.

"Your appointment is here." He leaned against the doorjamb. "I think I scared her off, but I have to put my two cents in. She's too scrawny to be a good cook or take care of this house."

"You just let me handle it. We might not have much of a choice. No one wants to be a live-in housekeeper anymore." She patted his arm as she passed.

Johnny followed Mama D to the front porch.

Lacy Goodwin kicked the front tire of her car.

"What's she doing?" Mama D asked.

"Beating up her beater." Johnny chuckled.

"Do you think she has anger issues? Maybe we should let her ease on down the road?"

"I'm guessing that might be a problem. Looks like she's having car trouble. She might also think she wasted her time coming here." Johnny stepped around his mom and headed toward the little lady. "Pop the hood. I'll take a look."

"I've got cables. I just need a jump." She reached in through the open window and pulled out a set of frayed jumper cables.

"You must be Lacy. I'm Dixie Baker." Mama D was right behind him. "I see you've met my son, Johnny. I'm sorry I didn't hear the door. Won't you please come in, so we can chat?"

"I…I'm not sure. Your house is real pretty, but it's a lot bigger than I expected."

"Oh, honey, you're young. You can handle it. Come on in and let's have a glass of sweet tea and at least talk. Johnny will see about your car." Mama D put her arm around Lacy and guided her toward the house.

Johnny lifted the hood and stared at the dusty old innards a long moment before he too kicked the tire.

Chapter Two

Almost on the verge of tears, Lacy sucked it up, refusing to let these people see her cry. She took a shaky breath, held it, then let it out slowly before she straightened her shoulders and spoke to Mrs. Baker. "I appreciate you taking the time to talk to me."

They walked to the house while the buffoon Mrs. Baker called a son tinkered with her car. Maybe he'd get it running and she could get the heck out of these backwoods.

Lacy had actually looked forward to the potential of working in a rural place, where she could be unknown, and no one would think to look for her. She really wanted a new job and a new start. But if signs were any indication, she'd have to chalk this interview up to experience gained.

Mrs. Baker asked Lacy to wait in the living room while she got their tea. Lacy took the opportunity to look around.

Family photos lined one whole wall. She'd definitely need a ladder to dust those. The ceiling height was at least twelve feet. One end of the space held the biggest television she'd ever seen. She supposed in a room this size, you'd need a big screen if you wanted to see it from far away.

The furniture was oversized, distressed leather. It could be bought that way, but as she examined the couch, she got the impression the wear patterns were hard earned.

"Here you go." Mrs. Baker handed her a glass of tea.

The weight of the glass told Lacy it was crystal, so she gripped it with both hands. It would cost way more than she could afford to replace.

Mrs. Baker perched on the edge of the sofa, looking like a real lady. "Now, I saw on your résumé that you've worked for a cleaning service for the last ten years."

"Yes, ma'am." Lacy tentatively sat, attempting to mimic Dixie Baker's posture, before she placed her drink on a coaster on the coffee table. "My cousin owns the cleaning service, and I've been helping her since I was sixteen."

"Did you help her after school and on weekends then?"

"No, ma'am. I was full-time." Lacy looked down and smoothed her wrinkled dress over her legs.

"You did finish high school, didn't you?" Mrs. Baker's forehead wrinkled.

"I got my GED." A bead of sweat broke out on Lacy's upper lip, even though the air conditioning was doing its job.

"Well, that's wonderful. Good for you." She made a gesture with her fist, lifting it as in victory.

Lacy examined the smiling woman, who seemed genuinely happy for her, and a little of the tension Lacy carried eased out of her shoulders. Using both hands, she took a sip of her tea. It near about had the consistency of syrup, like sweet tea ought to have.

"What kind of cooking experience do you have?" Mrs. Baker asked.

"Well, I've been living with my cousin for the past few years and helping take care of her kids. I make supper most nights because Trina works a second job. Her new boyfriend's a cook at Applebee's, and he's been showing me how to fix some things, you know, to make it healthier?"

"That's kinda what we have in mind. My husband, Dan, suffered a heart attack a couple years ago, and well…our housekeeper, who recently retired, cooked traditional Southern fare. Lard makes everything taste better, don't ya know?" Mrs. Baker laughed.

Lacy smiled and nodded. Bobby had introduced her to extra virgin olive oil and I Can't Believe It's Not Butter, but nothing beat Crisco.

"Anyway," Mrs. Baker continued, "we *all* need to eat a little healthier and lose a few pounds. The men in the house will complain, so just be prepared for that. I figure we can save the pigging out for holidays and special occasions."

"How many people live here?"

"My husband and I are the only full-time

residents of this main house. But Johnny, who you've met, and his son, Nick, live in one of the cottages on the estate. You'd be cooking for the four of us most of the time. Well, five counting you. Together, Dan and I have six kids and eleven grandkids, and they're here most holidays, weekends, and any time school's out."

Lacy couldn't add that quickly in her brain, but it sounded overwhelming. "No wonder you need such a big house."

Mrs. Baker smiled. "The main house here has seven bedrooms, four full and two half baths. We also have three cottages. Johnny and Nick live in the two-bedroom cottage. The others just have one bedroom. If you come to work with us, you'd stay in one of those, and you can choose which one. Come on, let me show you around." Mrs. Baker stood.

While they toured the main house, Johnny came in.

His large hands were covered in dirt and grease. It was caked under his fingernails. "I need to run to the auto parts store in town. Mama D, can you get Nick off the bus if I'm not back?"

"Sure, honey. Go ahead."

He didn't discuss it with Lacy, and since it was her car, she was about to speak up when Mrs. Baker took her arm and guided her up the stairs. When Lacy glanced back, Johnny was gone.

After showing Lacy the bedrooms, bathrooms, and playroom on the second floor, Mrs. Baker led her out the back door onto a huge porch, which held half a dozen rocking chairs and two porch swings.

The view consisted of a big pool. Actually, there were two pools and what Lacy assumed was a hot tub. She'd heard about them, of course, but had never been in one.

"The smaller pool's for the younger kids," Mrs. Baker said. "Johnny's in charge of the outbuildings."

To the right stood a monster garage with six doors. To the left, there was a red barn, just like in the postcard pictures. A couple of horses milled around, and two bulldogs trotted in their direction.

Mrs. Baker shrieked. "That darn Houdini is an escape artist." She headed toward the barn. "Honey, you get these other horses back into the corral. I'll go after the troublemaker."

Lacy looked around to see if there was another person named Honey somewhere close by. She'd never been around horses and had no idea how to make them go back into their pen. One of the dogs sat by her feet, panting. The other dog had followed Mrs. Baker, so Lacy bent and scratched the pooch behind the ears.

"Can't you herd them or something?" she asked the dog whose lower jaw jutted out revealing sharp canine teeth.

She took a few steps toward a horse that picked its head up and looked at her. Waving her arms toward the open gate like she'd seen flight attendants do on television, she nodded her head in that direction. "Hey, horsey. You can just go on in. Shoo. Get in the pen. Come on." She clicked her tongue.

The horse bent his head back down to the grass

it munched on, ignoring her. That was nothing new. Lacy had been ignored most of her life, which was fine by her.

"Come on, Mr. Ed. You've got to get back in the pen." She motioned with her hand to no avail.

Lacy gasped in horror as a horse who was already inside the pen, started heading toward the open gate. "Oh no, you don't."

She went to close the gate and an amazing thing happened. The two horses outside the enclosure followed her. So did the dog.

"That's right, go on in." She closed the gate behind the second horse and secured it with a bungee cord she found on the ground.

Leaning against the fence, she let out a long breath. Something pulled her hair and she turned. The horse she'd called Mr. Ed was laughing at her. She reached around to her ponytail and found it damp with horse spit.

"Gross." She wiped her hands on her dress as Mrs. Baker appeared, horseless.

"Lacy, honey, hop on that golf cart and go pick Nick up at the end of the driveway. I've got to go inside and call Dan. I lost that darn horse."

Lacy looked at the golf cart. She'd never been in one. It was turning into a day of firsts.

After she slid behind the wheel, the dog climbed on board and sat in the floor, staring up at her.

"I don't suppose there's an operator's manual lying around," she said to the canine.

She turned the key to the On position. Nothing happened. She turned it off and then on again. Still nothing. Maybe it was like Bessie, and you had to give it a little gas. She turned it off and then on and hit the gas. The cart shot forward in a lurch, almost smashing into the barn. Yelling, she jerked the wheel away from the red wooden building.

Once her heart left her throat and returned to her chest, she took a deep breath and pressed the gas pedal more gently. The cart moved forward. She let off the pedal and it slowed to a stop. After stopping and starting several times, she sort of got the hang of it. However, the dog looked a little green.

"Sorry, buddy, but I've never been on a farm or anything. They don't have these things at the trailer park where I live. Though they should." She'd never had much to smile about in her life, but as she caught a little wind in her hair, the rare expression settled on her face.

Before she got to the end of the long driveway, she came across a young boy walking toward her. She let off the accelerator and coasted to a stop near him.

"Do you know how to drive this thing?" she asked.

"Yes, ma'am." His little voice and polite manners made her grin bigger.

"Good. You can drive us back to the house. I made the dog car sick and myself too, a little." She slid over to the passenger side and crossed her legs in the seat, since the dog took up the floorboard.

"Who are you?" His hands gripped the straps of his book bag.

"I'm Lacy. I was interviewing for the

housekeeper job, but the horses got out and your Grandma sent me to get you because she had to call somebody."

"I'm Nick." He extended his hand. "Nice to meet you."

She shook his hand. "You too. Will I get in trouble for letting you drive?"

Nick tossed his backpack on the rack behind the seat and took the wheel. "No, ma'am. They don't let me drive on the road, but I can drive on the property."

After making a tight turn, which came very close to a tall pine tree, Nick headed for the house. "Where's my dad?"

"I think he went to get a part for my car. It's kind of a pain. Only runs when it wants to." She shrugged.

"Was it Houdini who got out?"

She told him what happened and then added, "One of the horses tried to eat my hair."

He laughed. "White horse with brown spots?" When she nodded, he continued. "That's Bo and that means he likes you. Jake there likes you too, or he wouldn't have gotten in the cart with you."

"I just thought he liked going for rides." She leaned to rub Jake's ears, and his tongue swiped her arm. By the time she got back to North Carolina, she'd be covered with all kinds of animal slobber.

"Scratch his jowls and he'll love you forever," Nick said.

She moved her hands down and around. The dog sniffed her a second before he leaned into her open fingers. What she hoped was a happy moan escaped from deep in the throat of the beast.

Nick parked the cart by the barn, and Lacy followed him into the house. Her white open-toe sandals revealed how dirty her feet had gotten. Between her sweat, the dry ground, and chasing animals, she needed some boots or something. No wonder Johnny had been wearing a pair.

She wiped her shoes thoroughly at the door before she went in, but it did nothing for her nasty feet. So much for impressing the lady doing the hiring.

Mrs. Baker was on the phone, and the doorbell rang. "Can you get that for me, honey?"

Lacy went to the door and opened it to an older well-dressed woman.

"Good afternoon. My name is Mavis Dunn. I'm here to interview for the housekeeper position."

"Please come in." Lacy showed Ms. Dunn to the living room where she'd waited earlier. "I'll let Mrs. Baker know you're here."

Chapter Three

When Johnny returned to Southland, another unfamiliar car was parked out front. He had pushed Lacy's crappy Pinto into one of the garage bays, so he could have access to tools.

Getting out of his truck, he turned toward Nick, who ran to him.

"Hey, Dad. Houdini's out. Me and Miss Lacy were about to go try to find him. You wanna help us?"

"Damn horse. Get some rope and I'll be right there."

Johnny took his bag of supplies into the garage and left them to go see about the new horse.

Lacy waited outside the open barn door, looking disheveled, her curly brown hair sticking out every which way. Her big brown eyes were wary as he approached.

Nick came out of the barn with rope and sat behind the wheel of the golf cart. Johnny smiled to himself. He had loved to drive when he was that age, too. It'd made him feel special when his dad had let him.

Johnny slid onto the passenger seat and took the nylon, working on a loop knot, so he could catch the horse when they found him.

"Are you coming, Miss Lacy?" Nick asked.

She stood beside the cart looking unsure. "I'll just stay here."

"Aw, come on, Miss Lacy." Johnny patted his legs. "You can sit in my lap."

"No, thanks." Her gaze fixed on her feet.

Johnny placed his palm on his forehead. "Bud, you better let me drive. You can sit on Miss Lacy's lap and knot the rope for me."

"Okay." Nick hopped out and ran around the cart as Johnny scooted behind the wheel.

"Come on. It'll be fun." Nick slapped the empty seat with a huge grin.

After a moment's hesitation, Lacy sat, and Nick perched on her legs and started knotting the rope.

"How'd you learn to do that?" Lacy asked Nick.

"My dad. He's real good at it. Hey, Dad, check where we feed the deer. Houdini may be over there looking for corn."

Johnny steered the cart down the dirt path, which led deeper into the woods. "I got a new battery and spark plugs, but it may be your starter." He flipped his palm up. "If that's the problem, I can't fix it, but I have a mechanic friend I can call."

"Was that your pink car in the garage?" Nick

asked her.

"It's supposed to be red." She sighed. "At least, it used to be, but it's so faded it does look kinda pink."

"It's okay to drive a pink car if you're a girl." Nick's face held a serious expression.

"Lucky for me." The slightest hint of humor tinged her voice.

"The problem isn't the color," Johnny said. "It's that it's a Ford. You know what that stands for, don't cha?"

"Trust me, I know," Lacy said.

"That's why we're Chevy people," Nick said.

"It was my Grandma's car, and I got it when she passed away."

"What year model is it?" Johnny asked.

"Seventy-nine. It was old when I got it."

"Somebody had to take care of it to keep it running all these years."

"One of Susan's boyfriends was a mechanic." After a pause, she said, "Susan's my mother."

"Where are you from? And why do you call your mother by her first name?" Johnny asked.

"Murphy…and it's none of your business." She looked the other way.

Johnny raised an eyebrow. "North Carolina's a long way to travel in that car."

"It made it here all right, on a wing and a prayer. There's a horse." She pointed.

Johnny slowed to a stop and took the rope from Nick.

"Can I try it, Dad?"

"Normally, I'd say yes, but I've got to get back

and see about Miss Lacy's car. You can get him next time. 'Kay, bud?"

"Okay. Watch this, Miss Lacy." Nick stood next to her.

Johnny walked purposefully in a line parallel to the horse. As he neared the beast, he started swinging his rope. The horse turned his head toward the sound, and with a flick of his wrist, Johnny sent the loop over the animal's head and pulled it tight.

Houdini tugged a little, but Johnny got him under control and called for Nick to bring the lead line, which he hooked onto the bridle. "You want to take him back to the barn, Nick?"

"Yes, sir." His boy smiled a big ole snaggled-tooth grin at him.

"Good man." He ruffled Nick's hair.

As Johnny drove the cart back to the house, he glanced at Lacy. "Whose car was out front?"

"Another lady interviewing for the job." Lacy stared straight ahead.

"Oh… Well, how do you feel about that?" He raised an eyebrow.

She shrugged. "Of course, she'll get it. But at least I'll have a good story to tell when I get home."

"Don't be so sure. I might just vote for you." He grinned.

***

Lacy supervised as Johnny replaced Bessie's battery, then spark plugs. She'd seen it done before, and he seemed to know what he was doing. Mainly, she watched *him*. Not only was he tall, he was brawny with broad shoulders and a thick chest. He wasn't all muscle though. He carried a few extra pounds around the middle, which reminded her of what Mrs. Baker had said about cooking healthy.

The skin on his arms showed off how much time he spent in the sun. She could get pretty tanned in the summer if she ever had the time to actually lay out and do nothing.

Dragging her eyes away from the flesh on his low back where his T-shirt had ridden up and his jeans hung low, she stopped staring.

"How much did all this stuff cost?" She held her breath, dreading the answer.

"Not much. I do a lot of business with them to keep my '84 Chevy pickup running, so they give me a discount." His deep voice echoed from under the hood.

"I can pay you back." *If you'll accept a post-dated check.* She grimaced.

"Let's worry about that later. This may all be for naught. Turn her over and see what happens."

Lacy got behind the wheel, engaged the clutch with her left foot, the brake with her right, made sure it was in neutral, said a prayer, and turned the key. Nothing. Maybe old Bessie had finally died.

Lacy's breath hitched in her chest as she fought back panic.

Hearing Johnny say something, she got out to find him on his cell phone. A moment later, he hung up.

"My buddy can't come by until the morning to take a look." He slid his phone into his back pocket. "I can take you home, or you can spend the night and drive back tomorrow. I was going to suggest that anyway since it's getting so late."

Lacy hadn't expected to be gone overnight. She didn't have any clothes or a toothbrush. It was only a two-hour drive, but it was too far to ask him to drive her there and back.

"Um, I need to call my cousin." She tried to smooth the wrinkles from the front of her dress.

Johnny walked beside her to the house. "You can use the land line 'cause cell reception can be spotty out here, unless you have the right carrier."

"I don't have a cell phone."

"What?" He looked her way, almost shouting.

She jumped away from him, but he didn't seem to notice.

Stopping, he turned to face her. "You mean to tell me you're driving around in a rust bucket on its last leg, and you don't have a way to call somebody if you break down?"

Lacy crossed her arms over her ribs. "I had a pre-paid one, but I ran out of minutes. Cell phones are a luxury, not a necessity. It's more important to put food on the table. If you had to choose between that and food for Nick, what would you pick?"

The question brought him up short, and while he worked his jaw, trying to form a response, he glanced from her to the ground and back. She took another side step to put distance between them.

"What are you two on about?" Mrs. Baker called from the porch. "I could hear you from inside."

Lacy furrowed her brow, not realizing they'd been yelling at each other. "Can I use your phone?"

"Of course, just dial one and the number. We have that free long distance, since some of our kids live out of the area." Mrs. Baker put her hand on Lacy's back, guiding her inside.

Lacy called her cousin, Trina, and took the portable phone out onto the back porch, since Mrs. Baker and Johnny had followed her inside.

"Hey, girl. How'd it go?" Trina asked.

"Terrible. Bessie's broken. A mechanic's supposed to come look at her in the morning." Lacy wiped at the moist corner of her eye.

"Are you spending the night?"

Lacy discussed her dilemma with her cousin, who encouraged her not to leave without her car. Trina couldn't be sure when she could drive Lacy back down there to retrieve it.

Lacy wasn't sure she could pay the mechanic or reimburse Johnny for the parts. Her checking account was low, and her savings had gone to help repair the air conditioner in Trina's trailer when it had gone out a few months before.

When Lacy disconnected the call, she rubbed her temples to ward off the headache starting there. She craved a cigarette and a Mountain Dew.

About then, a truck pulled into the garage. A man got out and thumped a cigarette out into the darkness.

When he spotted Lacy, he said, "I'd appreciate it if you wouldn't tell anyone what you just saw. With my heart condition, they'd spank me if they found out."

The man was so big she doubted anyone could spank him.

"If I could bum one from you, I'd be much obliged," she said.

He turned back to the garage and came out with a cigarette and a lighter.

"Thanks." She held it between her fingers. "I was trying not to smoke before my interview today, so I wouldn't smell like it, you know? But I doubt I'm on the short list, so what the hell?" She put the filter in her mouth, struck the lighter, and inhaled deeply. Her shoulders dropped, and her head rolled back as she exhaled.

"I'm Dan Baker," the man said, taking his lighter from her. "And who might you be?"

"I might be Lacy Goodwin, though some days I wish I weren't." She chuckled and explained why she was there, about her car, her overnight stay, the horses, and Mavis Dunn.

The door opened and Johnny stepped out onto the porch followed by Nick.

"Hey, Big Daddy." Nick ran and threw his arms around her cig carrying savior.

"Dad," Johnny said. "I see you've met Lacy."

Lacy tried to hide her cigarette behind her skirt, especially from the little boy.

"Yeah, she was just telling me about her exciting visit to Southland," Dan said.

"Do you have another cancer stick?" Johnny asked.

It took Lacy a moment to realize he was speaking to her.

"Oh…ah…this is my last one." She held it out to him. "Here. Take it. I don't want to smoke around Nick. Secondhand smoke is bad news."

Hesitating with his mouth in a thin line, Johnny took the half-smoked cigarette and looked at her curiously before he took a drag.

"Firsthand smoke is bad too, Miss Lacy and Daddy," Nick said. "Everybody needs to quit."

"I've quit a bunch of times," Lacy said.

"Me too," Dan said.

"Me three." Johnny put the cigarette out on the sole his boot.

"If you come live here, Miss Lacy, I'll help you quit," Nick said. "Since you don't want to smoke around me, I'll stay with you all of the time. Except when I'm at school…or asleep…or in the bathroom."

Lacy laughed. "You're the sweetest thing, Nick. I guess I better go help with dinner or else I definitely won't get the job."

In the kitchen, she found Mrs. Baker thawing chicken in the microwave.

"I need to wash up, but then I'm happy to make dinner," Lacy said.

When she saw herself in the mirror of the half bath next to the laundry room, she nearly shrieked.

She used paper towels to wipe off. Bathing in front of the sink was nothing new. It happened a lot growing up because either the hot water heater didn't work or her mom didn't pay the water bill. A whore's bath is what Trina always called it. Many years passed before Lacy had understood what that meant.

Her flyaways were unruly, so she fixed her hair. Loose strands in their food would ensure she didn't get the job.

She was considering a hair net as she exited the bathroom to find four sets of eyes staring at her.

Chapter Four

Johnny propped his elbows on the counter and covered his mouth, trying not to smile at the startled expression on Lacy's face. When Mama D said Lacy was probably taking a bath in the sink, he'd thought she was joking.

The little lady cleaned up nice.

"Sorry that took so long," Lacy said. "Rounding up horses isn't exactly a dirt-free experience."

"Don't worry about it, honey," Mama D said. "Now don't feel any pressure, but we'd love to see what you can do in the kitchen. Sort of like a working interview."

"Yeah, no pressure," Johnny added, since they were literally bellied up to the bar. "We're just going to sit here and watch you work your magic."

Nick giggled, and Lacy crossed her eyes at him, which made Johnny smile and Nick snort.

"Is there anything y'all don't eat?" Lacy asked.

"We eat anything that doesn't eat us first," Big Daddy said. "How do you feel about venison?"

"Yum," she said.

"When the season opens, we'll get you one."

"Or two," Johnny said.

"Or three," Nick joined in.

The thawed chicken rested in the sink, so Lacy searched the refrigerator and cupboard for sides and seasonings. She pulled out garlic, rosemary, red potatoes, and green beans. Trying to ignore her audience, she got to work.

"It's a good thing you're not shy, Lacy." Big Daddy sipped his tea.

"Actually, I *am* kind of shy, but I'm getting better as I get older." She never looked up as she spoke.

"Have you ever been married?"

Johnny cleared his throat. "Mama D, I don't think you're supposed to ask that in a job interview."

"Well, if we hire her, she'll be family, like May and Ben Hill were. We should know things about her. Do you want her around Nick if she might be crazy in the head?"

"She's not crazy in the head," Nick said.

"The fact that she doesn't want Nick to inhale secondhand smoke tells me all I need to know about her." Johnny rattled the ice in his glass.

"Um, hello. I'm right here, even though you're talking about me like I'm not." Lacy folded a dishtowel with shaky hands. "I'm starting to think y'all are the crazy ones."

"You'd be right about that, Miss Lacy." Big

Daddy grinned and tipped his glass to her.

She cleared her throat. "My ex-boyfriend might claim me as his common law wife. And you," she gestured to Johnny with the tip of the knife she was using to cut potatoes, "you shouldn't judge me on so little information. If Nick was mine, I'd be very careful who I let around him. You're doing a good job with him, but he's young and trusting. It's your job to protect him from the crazies."

The more she spoke, the more Johnny liked her. Her priority was the safety of his son, and she'd only just met him. Even if she was skinny and a bad cook, he'd vote for her.

"So not married then?" Johnny grinned.

Her lips twisted, suppressing a smile he guessed. She rolled her eyes, giving him a shit-for-brains look. He was used to that. People often thought he was funny and a little dumb. Maybe he was. He'd sure lived up to the reputation many times without meaning to.

"No, not married. No kids that I know of. Only a mother and a couple of cousins." She slid the roasting pan into the oven and turned to the fridge.

"How tall are you?" Johnny asked.

She raised an eyebrow and looked over her shoulder. "Five, two. How tall are you?"

"Six, two."

Lacy set out five bowls and ingredients for salad.

"You mentioned your mom. What about your dad?" Mama D asked.

"He died when I was little…in prison." Her gaze focused on the mushrooms she sliced.

Johnny cut his eyes to his dad whose brows climbed under the brim of his ball cap. She'd gotten their attention.

"Prison?" Mama D spread her palms on the counter. "What for?"

"Manslaughter. He killed someone while drunk driving." Her hands were shaking, so she paused to wipe them on the borrowed apron she was wearing.

"My first husband killed himself drunk driving," Mama D said.

Lacy looked at her, and Johnny sensed a connection forge between them in that moment. His dad put an arm around Mama D and pulled her to his side, kissing her cheek.

When Johnny looked from his parents to Lacy, there was a faraway look in her eyes. For a second, a small smile graced her rosy lips, and she almost hugged herself.

Longing.

He recognized it because he felt it too. Wanted what his parents and siblings had with their spouses.

When Lacy caught him staring, she quickly returned to her task. Johnny silently exhaled as he looked down and squeezed the back of his neck.

"Do you have chocolate chips?" Lacy held a carton of raspberries.

Nick slid off of his stool and went to the pantry. Leave it to his kid to know the location of the chocolate chips. Nick also helped Lacy get the dishes and silverware and set the table.

When they all sat to dinner, they had to convince Lacy to join them. She wanted to eat her meal in the kitchen, apart from the family.

"May and Ben Hill always ate with us," Mama D explained.

"Yeah, they were like our family," Nick said.

"That's true," Johnny said. "Aunt May raised me since I was born. She was here at Southland before Mama D."

Lacy set her plate down and slid into a chair. "So, you miss her?"

There were nods all around, but her gaze was on Johnny who offered her a closed mouth smile.

"This tastes real good." Nick chewed his chicken with his mouth open.

"Smaller bites, son," Johnny said and gestured a closed signal with his hand.

"It's delicious." Big Daddy held up his fork. "I admit when I saw how petite you were, I assumed you couldn't cook, but I stand corrected."

"Speaking of petite, I advise you to take small bites and chew thoroughly," Lacy said. "There won't be seconds…but there *is* dessert."

Johnny grinned at his dad who returned the expression. They liked dessert.

When Lacy set small plates of raspberries stuffed with chocolate chips in front of them, they eyed each other.

"Where's the rest?" Johnny asked.

Lacy bit her lip. "Chew slowly and savor each bite."

Johnny tried, but each bite tasted more delicious than the last and left him wanting more. More dessert…and more Lacy.

***

Lacy received a lesson from Mrs. Baker on

how to start the dishwasher. Who knew those appliances could be so high-tech? They still hand washed dishes at home.

"Now, do you want to sleep here in the main house or in one of the cottages?" Mrs. Baker asked with smiling eyes.

Lacy folded her apron. "What's most convenient for you, Mrs. Baker? Of course, I'll clean up after myself before I go, but I don't want to be any trouble."

"Please, call me Dixie or Mama D like the kids."

"Um…I'm not sure. Maybe, if I work here, after a while, I might can call you by your first name." Lacy stared at her clasped hands.

"I need to speak with Dan, but I'm almost certain you'll be our choice, Lacy."

She looked up. "What about Mavis Dunn?"

"She wants to be off on holidays. That's when I need help the most, don't cha know?"

"Oh, well, my family isn't big on holidays. For Christmas, I usually get a carton of cigarettes from Su—my mother. My cousin and I always give each other pajamas—the kind you actually sleep in, not the kind you only wear for a minute before they end up on the floor."

Mrs. Baker laughed. "I know exactly what you mean. Speaking of, let me get you something to sleep in and a toothbrush."

Lacy rubbed her tongue across her teeth. *Ick.* A toothbrush sounded like a real good idea.

Mrs. Baker returned with the items. "Why don't I show you the cottages and you can decide where you want to sleep?"

After a short ride in the golf cart, they went into the first cabin. It had a very masculine feel, with leather and dark wood everywhere. The second cabin had white-washed wooden furniture and neutral colors, like something from *Southern Living* magazine. If Lacy had a place of her own and could afford to decorate, it'd look something like this cozy cottage.

She stood in the door to the bedroom and spun in a slow circle. "I'll stay here. I-if that's okay?"

While she'd cooked dinner, the bundle of nerves in the pit of her stomach had reminded her of an out-of-balance washing machine. In the quiet of the small cabin in the woods, they had settled to a minor vibration.

"Wonderful. Do you need anything else before I go?"

"Um. What time should I have breakfast ready?"

"Seven, and thanks, Lacy. You're a real peach." Mrs. Baker hugged her.

Lacy got in the shower. And when she was done, she took the body wash to her clothes since they smelled like horses and sweat. After finding wire hangers in the closet, she hung her dress and undies up in the doorway between the bathroom and the bedroom. She turned the ceiling fan on high and prayed they'd be dry by morning.

In the borrowed nightshirt, with wet hair and chattering teeth, she added an extra quilt to the bed, and then slid under the heavy weight of the covers.

Moments after she switched out the light,

someone knocked on the door.

She peeked out the window, but didn't see anyone in the light from the front porch. When she opened the door, she found a treat.

***

The next morning, Lacy had a bowl of fruit alongside spinach and cheese omelets on the table at seven. She perched on a barstool and sipped black coffee, craving a cigarette to go with it. If the nicotine fairy hadn't paid her a visit the night before, she wouldn't have any smokes to tempt her. Now she had a pack minus one, and a lighter.

Sighing, she settled for the warm drink instead. She'd have to get used to it if she intended to quit for real. Nick's offer to help her made her grin. She loved kids, but she was glad she'd never had any. She didn't want them growing up like she had.

The back door opened, and Nick rushed in. "Good morning, Miss Lacy."

Johnny was right behind him. "Good morning, Miss Lacy."

"Good morning." She stood. "What can I get you to drink?"

Nick slammed her with a hug, and she staggered to catch her balance.

"Easy, son." Johnny reached for a mug. "I'll get coffee, thanks."

"Chocolate milk, please," Nick said. "Ooh, you made real food for breakfast. I usually eat cereal or a pop tart on school days."

"Oh," she said. "I thought I might still be on a working interview, so I went all out."

"We'll take it. Won't we, bud?" Johnny took

the seat next to Nick. "Are you joining us?"

She slid into a chair across the table from them. "Should I wake your parents?"

Johnny checked his watch. "They'll be out in a minute. Nick, you wanna say grace?"

Lacy smiled at the idea of a family who prayed over their meals together. The night before Mr. Baker had said it. Lacy hoped no one would ask her to say it, because all she knew was the *God is Great* blessing from childhood.

Mr. and Mrs. Baker joined them, and after praising her cooking, Mrs. Baker spoke. "Lacy, we'd like to offer you the job."

"Really?" Her face warmed as her heart thumped against her ribs.

"I realize you have some concerns about the size of the house, but May always broke it down into smaller jobs. You don't have to do the entire house every day. You'll have a credit card to purchase anything you need from groceries to cleaning supplies. We'll pay you by direct deposit. You do have a checking account, don't you?"

Lacy nodded, but she was still having a hard time processing the fact they wanted her for the job. *A credit card?* They trusted her with a credit card, and she could buy what she needed to do her job better. She needed healthy recipes.

"Is there a library in town?" Lacy asked. "They usually have cookbooks."

"Honey, just go online and buy whatever you need. You can use my credit card until we get you your own," Mrs. Baker said.

Lacy opened her mouth and then closed it,

unsure what to say.

Johnny laughed. “I think she’s in shock.”

“How soon can you start?” Mrs. Baker asked.

“Ah…how soon do you need me?”

“Yesterday.” Mr. and Mrs. Baker and Johnny all spoke in unison.

A second later, the doorbell rang.

“That’ll be Max to see about your car.” Johnny slid his chair away from the table. “Will you take Nick to meet the bus?”

Lacy got to her feet. As she followed Nick out the back door, he turned and took her hand. “I voted for you too. We all did.”

Lacy swiped at her eyes to brush away the tears barely being held back by her lashes before she settled onto the seat of the golf cart. “Will you teach me to drive this stupid thing?”

Chapter Five

Johnny took Max to the garage. "Whatever the cost to repair, I'm paying. If the little lady asks, tell her it's a freebie or something."

"You got it, man." Max poked around under the hood. "Help me push it out, and I'll tow it to the shop. Probably have it ready tomorrow."

"Great," Johnny said, his voice dripping sarcasm.

Once Max left, Johnny headed toward the barn to start the chores. He was avoiding Lacy because she wasn't going to be happy. He grabbed a shovel and glanced inside the first stall. He'd better talk to her before he got covered in muck.

After striding to the house, he found her cleaning up breakfast dishes.

"I can take you home later today. And if you'll be bringing your clothes and stuff, we can haul it in my truck."

"Ah…I hadn't thought that far ahead." She bit

her lower lip. “I don’t really have much. Just some clothes and makeup.”

One corner of his mouth turned up. “You don’t need makeup.”

“Um, Johnny.” She squared her shoulders and looked at him. “I haven’t accepted the job yet, and before I do, I need to tell you somethin’.”

“Uh-oh. What did I do now?” His face warmed as he mentally placed a palm to his forehead. *You know what you did, dumbass.*

“It makes me uncomfortable when you comment on my appearance, especially my size.”

He looked down a second before he met her gaze. “I’m sorry. I promise not to call you a shrimp, if you promise not to call me an ogre.”

“You’re not an ogre.” Her shy smile made his chest tighten.

“I fool around a lot.” He shrugged. “I don’t mean anything by it.”

“Okay,” she said. “And thanks for offering me a ride.” She scratched her head. “I still need to figure out what to do.”

“I’ll be in the barn. Come get me if you need me.”

“Wait. Do you work at an office?” she asked.

He propped a hand on the counter by the sink. “I used to work with the family business, but I’d rather work outside. When Uncle Ben Hill retired, I took over the care of Southland. I also farm trees.”

“What’s the family business?” She dried a coffee cup.

“Home health supplies and services.”

She nodded, looking pensive as she folded the

dishtowel. “Hey, I forgot to ask your mom, but is there like a uniform or dress code?”

Johnny bit his tongue, so he wouldn’t tell her she had to wear a French maid’s outfit. He would need to watch the flirting, since the last thing he needed was a sexual harassment lawsuit. And he didn’t want to make her uncomfortable.

“Aunt May always wore a dress and apron, just like what you’re wearing now. Oh, and support hose and those thick-soled shoes that little old ladies wear.” He grinned.

“I’ll definitely wear sturdier shoes. Maybe not old lady sturdy.” She stuck her foot out. “These were meant for a sit-down interview, not a working one.”

“Kick ‘em off. We aren’t formal around here.” He headed for the door.

After lunch, Lacy told him she was ready to go get her things, so Johnny pulled his newer truck out of the garage for the four-hour road trip.

“Y’all have a lot of vehicles,” she said.

“There are a lot of us.” Johnny spent the drive to North Carolina telling her about his brothers and sisters, their spouses, and kids.

Just after they crossed the state line, she directed him to a lane, which snaked through a trailer park. He drove slowly down the bumpy, rutted out drive, while taking in the condition of the mobile homes.

Most were in decent shape, but one or two looked like a strong wind could blow them over. The mildew covered siding on several homes had his fingers itching to get his pressure washer up there. But then, there was the whole knocking someone's house down thing.

He cleared his throat. "You could throw a rock and hit Georgia."

"I know. It's this one." She pointed to a double wide, which appeared to be fairly well taken care of. Some of the skirting around the bottom was missing, and a furry-eared feline poked its head out a second before disappearing into the shadows.

He parked his truck then followed her inside, trying to be nonchalant about not having been in a trailer house in many years. With the exception of a few dishes in the sink, everything was tidy. The carpet was well worn, and the Formica countertop had more than its share of nicks and chips.

A few moments after she went down the hallway lined with dark paneling, he stalked after her, his weight making the floors creak in protest.

In a small bedroom, she pulled an old beat-up suitcase from under the lower bunk bed.

"You live here with your cousin and her kids?" He leaned against the door frame.

"For the last three years. I've been sharing this room with Annie; she's six. Thomas has his own room next door. He's eight." She dusted a spider web off the luggage with her hand.

"Where did you live before?"

"With my boyfriend." She opened a dresser drawer and started packing her clothes.

"What happened? You wise up and dump him?" He crossed his arms over his chest.

"Something like that." She pulled open another drawer. "Annie will be glad to have her own room again."

"I bet you will, too."

"Sharing wasn't so bad. I've helped take care of her since she was a baby." A sweet smile lit up Lacy's face.

"She'll miss you then."

"Yeah, but it's not too far. When Bessie's working again, I can come see them sometimes."

"What about your mama?" Johnny asked.

Her back stiffened. Then she shrugged. "I'm not her favorite person, and she's not mine."

"But still, she's your mama. You should at least try."

"You don't know what you're talking about, Johnny." She raised her voice then just as quickly, softened it. "Leave it alone."

For the time being, he'd do as she wished. But his curiosity was piqued. With the closeness of his family, he couldn't understand when people didn't get along with their relatives. Had to be a story there. Probably not a good one. Maybe, when she knew him better, she'd open up and share.

***

Sweat formed above Lacy's upper lip. Her face needed to release some of the heat, which had begun to build as they'd gotten closer to Trina's house. All she could think was that privileged Johnny was about to see how the other half lived.

If he'd been shocked, it didn't show on his face. At least, she didn't think it had because she could barely look at him for trying to conceal the flush running up her neck. Compared to the mansion his family owned, shoot even compared to the little cabins at Southland, the only thing opulent about Magnolia Estates Mobile Home Park was the name.

Her embarrassment gave way to anger when he asked about her mother and judged her. She had no intention of telling him about the loser who'd given birth to her. Popping out a baby didn't make someone a mother.

Thankfully, he'd dropped it, and eventually, she stopped grinding her teeth. She'd known Johnny less than twenty-four hours and had already learned subtlety didn't work with him.

On the drive back to Southland, she bit her lip and stared out the window, trying to figure out what on earth to wear when she worked. While at home, she'd changed into jeans, a T-shirt, and sneakers. She'd gotten the pants at Goodwill, and they'd already had a small hole in one knee. It was a struggle to keep from picking at it. What she had on wouldn't be nice enough to work in. She didn't have many dresses, and she certainly never wore them to clean houses. Her uniform while working with Trina was cut off sweatpants and a tank top. Maybe when she got her first paycheck, she could go buy some cotton dresses that looked okay with tennis shoes. If she had any money left after fixing Bessie.

"You okay?" Johnny rested one hand on the steering wheel and angled his shoulders toward her.

"I'm a little nervous, I guess." She rubbed her hands together. "I've never lived anywhere else."

"If you ever get homesick, it's just a hop, skip, and a jump back to NC."

A slow heat crept up from her chest, so she barely glanced at him. "You're sweet. Thanks for making me feel better."

Johnny drove her to the cottage and helped her unload her things. Since it had taken them all afternoon to go to Murphy and back, unpacking would have to wait until after supper.

Checking her dollar store wrist watch, she waited until Johnny'd been gone five minutes before she walked to the main house. If she cut through the woods, she could get there faster. There were obvious trails between some of the trees, but she decided to stick to the main path. It should only take about five or ten minutes.

As she walked, she took in the pretty and peaceful surroundings. There were woods all around where she'd grown up, but even so, there'd never been solitude. She'd been looking for a remote place, and she'd found it at Southland.

When Lacy got to the kitchen, Nick was sitting at the counter doing his homework.

"Hey, cutie. Did you have a good day at school?" She ruffled his hair.

"Yes, ma'am." He slid off the stool and hugged her around the waist.

A sting pricked her eyes as she hugged him back. Nick made her feel welcomed. Kids had a way of showing you what they really thought with their actions, whereas adults normally hid behind polite words and white knuckles from keeping it all in.

The back door opened and Johnny came in. "Hey, kid. Where's *my* hug?"

Nick went to his dad, who picked him up in a bear hug then slung him over his shoulder.

"Miss Lacy, I seem to have misplaced my sack of taters. Have you seen it around here anywhere?" Johnny made a show of looking around for something.

Nick giggled. "I'm right here, Dad."

She couldn't help but smile as the boys horsed around. There was no doubt Johnny loved his son. For a brief moment, Lacy wondered about the mom, but with her own mama drama, she left well enough alone.

Chapter Six

Just over a week later, Lacy waited at the end of the driveway for Nick to get off the school bus. She was settling in, and she'd almost set up a routine for taking care of such a huge place.

Bessie had returned from the dead, but what bothered Lacy was Max's unwillingness to let her pay him. He'd said it was just a loose cable, and he couldn't charge her for something it only took a twist of the wrench to fix. It made things awkward when he asked her out to dinner. Using her new job as an excuse, she'd declined, saying she didn't want to ask for time off yet. The truth was, she wasn't interested in dating him…or anyone else.

When the big yellow box of steel on wheels screeched to a stop, Nick lumbered off with droopy shoulders. To cheer him up, she almost let him drive the cart, but he'd been telling her she needed the practice. He tossed his book bag on the rack and slid in next to her, adjusting his legs to accommodate Jake the bulldog.

"How was your day?" She smoothed his hair.

"Fine." His lower lip poked out.

"Well, what's wrong then?"

He aimed those sad green eyes right at her. "I have to go spend the weekend with my mom in Atlanta."

"Atlanta sounds fun. I've been there once to Six Flags." Turning the wheel, she pressed the pedal.

"Six Flags is fun, but my mom doesn't usually take me places. Sometimes, I think I'm more of a nuisance than anything else."

A stab of pain shot through Lacy. No child should ever feel like they're a burden to their parents.

"Is your mom busy with work or something?"

"Her boyfriend. She usually gets a babysitter, so they can go out and party. When dad told her he wanted me to live with him here at Southland, she didn't even argue. She was glad to get rid of me." He scratched Jake under the chin.

"Nick, you're one of the coolest kids I know. I'm sorry your mom seems too busy for you, but maybe that'll change. Sometimes grownups can be selfish, and they don't think about how their actions affect other people. I wish I could make it better." Oh, Lord. She'd said too much. If she put the golf cart in reverse, could she also rewind and take her words back?

"Thanks," Nick said.

"When will you be back?" she asked, trying to look at the bright side, or at least point it out to him.

"Sunday. Do you want to come to movie night with me and my dad when I get home?"

"Will there be popcorn?" She raised her eyebrows.

"Yes, ma'am." His gap-toothed smile tugged at her heart.

"As long as it's not a scary movie, I'm in."

Right after she parked the cart, Johnny came out of the barn. "Hey, bud. You ready to go see the wicked witch of the East?"

After he'd sent Nick to their cottage to get his things, Johnny tilted his chin down toward her. "I can see that twisted mouth of yours. If you have something to say to me, just say it."

"It's not my place," she said, knowing she needed to walk away.

"But you're dying to say it anyway, aren't you?"

She almost backed down. Almost turned and ran, but for Nick's sake, she had to say something.

"My opinion might not count for anything, but I don't think you should badmouth Nick's mom in front of him."

He put his fists on his hips. "Since you're an expert on mothers, tell me why not."

Trying not to be obvious, she inched back. His words hurt, but not as much as his knuckles would if they made contact with her face.

She swallowed around the lump in her throat and focused on Nick. "For one, it teaches him it's okay to disrespect her. For another, he already has problems with her, and some of them may be mixed up with your feelings for her."

"Did he talk to you?" He adjusted his ball cap. "What did he say?"

Nick yelled something as he ran toward them, a different backpack swinging from his hand.

"We can talk later," she said.

"Will you ride to Atlanta with us?" he asked. "We'll be going against traffic, so it'll only take forty-five minutes to get there."

"I better not. I have to make dinner and start sorting through Halloween decorations. I hear the Bakers throw the biggest party around." She forced a smile.

Even though it was still September, she wanted to be ready for October. It'd be her first big decorating challenge, and maybe if she avoided Johnny, he'd figure out how to talk to Nick on his own.

***

After dropping Nick off at the house in Atlanta Johnny had once shared with Tiffany, he considered Lacy's reproof all the way back to Willow Creek. It'd been hard not to think about her words on the drive over, but he'd wanted to make the most of his time with Nick and do his best not to belittle his ex.

They'd talked about Nick's karate lessons and how much he missed his cousins, Josh and Jenny, who'd lived at Southland for almost a year before Maddie had remarried. They only lived five miles away now, but Nick had loved having them there all the time.

Johnny hadn't wanted to have just one child, since he enjoyed being part of a big family himself. But Tiffany hadn't wanted more, and it wasn't like

Johnny could force her.

Right after they'd separated, he'd tried to be very careful what he said around Nick. As time passed, he relaxed his diligence, and now Nick might be suffering from it somehow.

God knew Johnny wasn't perfect, but when it came to his son, he wanted to be the best dad he could be. His own dad was a good example of what a father should be, and Johnny did his best to emulate him.

While he stopped to pick up a twelve pack of beer, the bottom fell out of the dark gray sky. He was soaked by the time he made it back into his truck, but still he smiled to himself. If this continued, they might be able to go out and get a little mud on the tires later.

When he got back to Southland, he went in the main house and put the beer in the fridge.

"Are those cold?" Big Daddy held up his hands. "Toss one over here."

Lacy was washing dishes. "I made you a plate, in case you haven't eaten yet."

"I'm hungry for some twelve ounce nutrition." Johnny popped the top on a beer.

She put tinfoil on his plate and slid it into the fridge, while he stood holding the door open for her.

"You want one?" he asked.

"No, thank you." She turned back to the sink.

"Dad, it's a frog strangler out there. I'm thinking—"

"I know what you're thinking, son," his dad interrupted. "We ought to see if the four wheel drive on the old Blazer still works."

“Let’s watch a movie first,” Mama D said. “That’ll give the ground a little more time to soak up the rain.”

One movie later, Lacy shook her head at them. “Y’all’s idea of a good time on a Friday night is to go mud boggin’?”

“Yep,” Big Daddy said. “You don’t have to be so formal. We call it muddin’. We’re taking my old SUV, so we can all fit.”

“What happens if we get stuck?” she asked.

“Come on, fraidy-cat,” Johnny teased. “Haven’t you ever had any adventures?”

“Not fun ones.” She followed them to the garage.

Johnny moved the front seat forward for her. “What kind of adventures did you have that weren’t fun?”

After she climbed in the back, he slid in next to her, and his parents got in the front. The engine roared to life, and a knot of excitement jiggled in Johnny’s stomach.

“One time, when I was nine,” Lacy said, “the cops raided Su—my mother’s boyfriend’s property because of the marijuana plants he was growing. I ran forever through the woods to the neighbor’s house ‘cause I was scared the cops would arrest me.”

Dead silence. Even Johnny, who always had a smart remark for everything, couldn’t think of a single thing to say. It was no surprise to hear she’d had it rough, but that was more than he expected.

“Well, we won’t do anything that’ll get us arrested,” Mama D said.

"If we get in a bind, our son-in-law is a highway patrolman and his dad's the sheriff. We can call in a favor." Big Daddy winked over his shoulder as he took the long driveway faster than wet conditions warranted.

"You have law-dogs in the family?" Her eyes were as big as saucers.

"Yeah, but don't worry," Johnny said. "Your background check came back clean."

Chapter Seven

Lacy's stomach flipped upside down at the mention of the law and background checks. It stayed unsettled due to the slipping and sliding of the old SUV down the slick dirt road. With the rain still coming down in buckets, she held on to anything she could find to keep her hands from shaking and to keep from landing in Johnny's lap.

"You're not gonna barf, are you?" Johnny asked.

After they'd stopped to change drivers three times, he was next to her in the backseat again. Everyone wanted a turn behind the wheel, all except Lacy. She'd seen a Chinese fire drill in a movie once, but she'd never experienced it for real. It was the only fun part so far.

"If you vomit, you have to drive," Mr. Baker said with humor in his voice.

The threat made her swallow the bile back down. She let out a long, slow breath and rolled her shoulders. Everyone else was having a good time; she should be too.

The radio blared "The Joker" by Steve Miller Band, and the Bakers sang at the top of their lungs. She joined in until they fishtailed and slid sideways down the road.

"Yeehaw," Johnny yelled and looked at her. "Think of it like a ride at the fair. You're safe." He patted her leg once.

Okay, that helped. NOT. The fair. Safe? Had he ever seen the people who worked at fairs? They were drinking class, like she'd grown up. Not much safety in that.

Johnny leaned close to her ear. "You were right about what you said earlier. I still want to talk about it later."

With those words, she forgot her fear of landing in a ditch. Not really meaning to, she lifted her chin a little, proud she hadn't backed down.

"Does Nick like muddin'?" she asked.

"Yeah, and if he saw you being a chicken, he'd tease you mercilessly."

"No, he wouldn't," she said. "He'd try to make me less scared."

"You've gotten to know my son pretty well, haven't you?" He reached for her hand, but Mr. Baker hit the brakes, and the vehicle slithered like a snake, skidding at an angle. Instead, Johnny's arm went in front of her to keep her from flying into the front seat. When they finally stopped, her right boob was in his hand.

"Okay, Lacy's turn to drive," Mr. Baker said, throwing the vehicle in park.

Johnny jerked his hand away. "Um, I didn't mean to do that."

She fought a smile. "Your dad made you cop a feel. I blame him, and I'm *not* driving."

Johnny came around to her side and scooted the front seat forward. As Lacy protested, Mrs. Baker slid in the back, Mr. Baker right behind her. Johnny picked Lacy up and manually placed her in the driver's seat. He ran around to the passenger side, and she tried to avoid looking in the rearview mirror. She'd thought she heard Mr. Baker talking dirty to his wife, and sure enough, they were making out like teenagers.

"Okay, put it in drive, and slowly press the accelerator," Johnny instructed.

"I can barely drive a golf cart, and you're trusting me with a big, heavy truck like this."

"Yep, I trust you." Johnny dipped his chin once.

They were still sitting diagonal across the road, so she kept the steering wheel straight and turned it when Johnny said to. Her knuckles ached from the death grip she had on the round plastic. The further she went, the more her shoulders relaxed. Of course, they were topping out at ten miles per hour. She stopped holding her breath, except for during the little slips before she got the truck straight again.

Just when she would've called it fun, the vehicle started a slow motion glide toward the water-filled ditch. She jerked the wheel, but it was too late. It actually happened fast, but in her mind, it was a chariots-of-fire race to the trench.

She hadn't even driven two miles.

When the truck stopped sliding, it rested at an almost forty-five degree angle with the passenger side in the ditch and water coming in under the door.

Wanting to move, but unable to get her body to cooperate, she sat stupefied and terrified. "You still trust me?" she asked, barely able to get the words out.

"Famous last words." He grinned.

She'd only been working for the Bakers a little over a week. Her first paycheck was supposed to be direct deposited that day. It'd be her last one, too. Resting her head on the hard plastic center of the wheel, the horn honked. She screamed and jumped.

Laughter bubbled up from the back seat. "Dan, you've never made me so wet before."

"Yes, I have, darlin'," Mr. Baker replied.

"TMI, people." Johnny grimaced. "Old people sex is so gross."

"Um," Lacy said. "How do we get out of the ditch?"

"You're gonna have to push, little one," Mr. Baker said. "I hope you're stronger than you look."

A nervous laugh escaped Lacy. "This will teach y'all to make me drive."

She opened the door and looked before she jumped out. Since her side of the vehicle was slightly suspended in the air, it was a long way down. Her feet sank several inches deep in the mud. Groaning, she dropped her head. She couldn't afford to buy new shoes.

Johnny made a few attempts to drive them out, but to no avail.

After he jumped down behind her, he patted her back. “Well done. You know how to get stuck right.”

He pulled out his cell phone and called someone. The rain had slowed to a drizzle, but Mr. and Mrs. Baker stayed in the SUV, steaming up the windows. Lacy guessed it was good that older people could still get hot for each other. It must be nice to be wanted by the one you love.

Half an hour later, a tractor came along and stopped beside them. Lacy was introduced to Heath, the Highway Patrolman in the family. He looked like he could be on the front of one of the *Muscle and Fitness* magazines Johnny subscribed to.

Taking a steadying breath, she shook his hand before he and Johnny got them out of the ditch.

When they got out of the Blazer, the elder Bakers straightened their clothes before they hugged and thanked Heath. Johnny got Lacy’s attention and rolled his eyes and then waggled his brows at her.

“Have you been drinking, Lacy?” Heath’s tone was serious.

Her heart beat in her throat. “N-no, sir.”

“I’m only messing with you.” He waved his hand in the air. “If you hang with these hoodlums, you’re liable to get pulled out of ditches from time to time. Maddie and I got stuck in this very vehicle when we were in high school.”

They waved goodbye, and Johnny drove them home. Lacy huddled in the front passenger seat, hugging herself. Since she was soaked through and chilled to the bone, she clenched her jaw to keep her teeth from chattering. They ached from the pressure.

When they parked at the house, Lacy said goodnight and started walking to her cabin. Mercifully, the rain had stopped.

"Honey, don't you want to come in and warm up?" Mrs. Baker asked.

"No, ma'am. I need to get out of these wet clothes and muddy shoes." She kept walking. "I'll see you in the morning." She threw a hand up.

"Do you want Johnny to build you a fire?"

"No thanks," she called over her shoulder.

After leaving her muddy shoes on the little stoop, she went straight to the bathroom for a hot shower. When hypothermia was no longer a serious threat, she donned her favorite flannel pajamas and stepped outside to smoke a much needed cigarette—still working on the pack her mysterious benefactor had left her first night at Southland.

***

Johnny hid behind an oak tree, spying on Lacy. He admitted to himself it was a little creepy, but he'd wanted to make sure she was okay. His mind kept replaying the fear on her face during and after the little accident. She'd been twitchy, like a cat trapped in a room full of rocking chairs. His heart had twisted at seeing her reaction, and he hadn't returned to normal just yet.

When she lit her cigarette and leaned against the front porch post looking more relaxed, he decided to go talk to her.

He made some noise as he approached. "Hey, can I bum a smoke?"

“Ah, sure.” She crossed her arms over her chest. “They’re probably yours anyway, but thanks for the loan.” She reached out with one hand to give him the pack and the lighter.

He lit up and propped a muddy boot on the second stair. “I’m sorry I made you drive. Are you okay?”

“Yeah.” She nodded. “Just embarrassed I guess. I hope the Blazer’s okay.”

“It’s nothing a little soap won’t fix. Stop worrying about the truck.” Johnny didn’t mention Max would have to pull the dent out, and it might need new paint.

“Please tell your dad I’ll clean it up for him tomorrow.”

Uh-oh. He took a drag and exhaled a white cloud. “I’ll tell him, but it won’t do any good. I’m the outside guy.” Before she could argue, he changed the subject. “Tell me what Nick said.”

She told him about their conversation. Compassion came off Lacy in waves, and Johnny stepped onto the bottom stair, moving nearer to the woman who treated his son so well.

He looked up at the cloud-covered night sky. “How did you get so wise?”

“School of hard knocks,” she said. “As you can probably surmise, my mom never won any Mother-Of-The-Year awards. I was a burden to her, and she never let me forget it. I don’t think it’s right that people can have kids and then make them feel like it was their fault for being born. There should be a test or something before you’re allowed to be a parent.” She squatted down to stub out her cigarette on the top step.

"If there was a test, I would've failed it."

She shook her head and stood, putting them closer to eye level. "No, you wouldn't. You're a great dad."

"Yet, just this afternoon, you pointed out something I was doing wrong."

"I didn't mean—"

"No," he interrupted, holding up a hand. "You were right. Thanks for pointing it out. One of my character flaws is that I usually speak and act before I think. That was how I wound up married to Nick's mom in the first place."

"You loved her though, right?"

Johnny didn't answer while he looked out into the dark woods and took a drag of his cigarette. He wanted to say no, but it would be a lie. It was hard to admit Tiffany had broken his heart when he figured out she loved his money more than she loved him. It shouldn't have surprised him because he wasn't the easiest guy to love.

"Yeah." He ran a hand through his hair. "Despite the protests of my family. They could see what I couldn't. Our relationship was ninety-five percent physical though. I loved that, but there was no real depth. I'm bad about getting physical with a woman too soon."

"You don't have to tell me. I've known you nine days, and you already made it to second base." She nudged him with her elbow, barely grazing his arm.

There were so many places he could go with the accidental boob grab situation, but all of them led to the gutter and Lacy kicking him off her porch.

"You can't beat yourself up over your past. You got a great kid out of it." She studied the half-burned cigarette between his fingers.

Wiping the smirk off his face, he cleared his throat. "Nick's the best thing that ever happened to me."

"You're really good with him." Her serious expression faltered as her mouth fell open. "Oh, hey. What time will the troops arrive tomorrow?"

"About ten. Are you ready to be completely overwhelmed?"

"No. But if they're as nice as you, I'll be okay."

A smile lifted his heated cheeks. She thought he was nice. Mental fist pump.

"They'll love you." He thumped his cigarette butt into the dirt. "Hey, you should go to the game with us. It's a lot of fun."

"About as much fun as sliding a truck into a ditch?" She smirked. "Thanks, but maybe another time. I've got plans of my own."

Chapter Eight

When Lacy got to the main house the next morning, she found a surprise. A small wrapped box with a bow and her name on it sat on the kitchen counter. She picked it up and looked around. No one was peeking out from behind a door or anything, but she put the gift back down and started breakfast.

She'd taken extra time with her hair and put on mascara and a little lip gloss. She would be meeting three of the other Baker children along with their spouses and kids. Wanting to make a good impression, she wore a polo-type shirt tucked into khaki pants with a brown fake leather belt. The old pair of kicks she sported had seen better days, but her regular sneakers were still wet from washing the mud off.

Mrs. Baker came in. "Good morning, Lacy."

"Good morning. Is Mr. Baker very mad at me?" She tucked her chin and closed her eyes.

"He's not angry at all. Honey, believe me when I tell you that wasn't the first time that truck's been in a ditch and it won't be the last." She pushed the package on the counter toward Lacy. "This is for you, don't cha know?"

"I…ah…" *I don't deserve it, whatever it is.* "Who's it from?"

"All of us. It's kind of a work related thing. I don't know why I wrapped it really. We just wanted you to have a surprise to open." Mrs. Baker waved her hand like it was no big deal before she reached for the coffee pot.

Despite her efforts to remain unaffected, a grin tugged at Lacy's lips. She opened the package and found a cell phone.

"Johnny can show you how to use it. Our numbers are already programmed in, so if you're out and you need us, just call. Or if you're at the store and I think of something I need, I can text you."

"I'll definitely need a lesson. I've heard of texting, but I've never done it." Lacy slid the phone into her back pocket. "Thank you."

She put breakfast on the table and checked the time. The Bakers ate later and bigger on Saturday mornings. Hoping she might get a chance to sneak to her cottage for a smoke before the family arrived, Lacy headed out the back door. The first carload of folks pulled up before she could get around the swimming pool, so she waited to say hello.

Paul, the youngest son, and his wife, Jen, got out. Their kids were Carly and Tyler, and they all wore Georgia Bulldog shirts and hats.

The next SUV unloaded the youngest Baker daughter, Maddie, and her husband, Heath, whom Lacy had met the night before. They had three kids, Jenny, Josh, and Sara Ann—all were dressed in their University of Georgia gear.

The Bakers were a good-looking family, not an ugly one in the bunch, but Lacy never said it out loud as she walked back into the main house with them.

Johnny came in to greet his family and had kids on both shoulders before he could sit down. Clearly, he was the *fun* uncle.

When he had a free hand, he reached into his back pocket and tossed something at Lacy. She caught a Georgia Bulldog ball cap, red with a black G on the front.

"Put that on, so you don't look so out of place, Little Bit." He did a double take. "Are you wearing makeup?"

She ignored his question and ducked into the bathroom to readjust her ponytail through the hole in the back. So much for fixing her hair, but this was better. Not having been a big football fan, she wasn't betraying a team by wearing UGA's colors.

She gazed at her reflection a moment before she used a tissue to wipe off the lip gloss. She felt stupid for trying to make herself look better.

When she exited the washroom, Katie, one of the middle Baker children, introduced herself and her husband Robert, who was a big wig at the Governor's office. Their kids were Beth and Bobby. Beautiful people—all of them. Polished and put together.

Now, she wished she still had on her lip stuff. Trying to fit in, Lacy stood up a little straighter.

Once everyone had eaten, they gathered together in the family room, and Lacy had a hard time remembering who was who. To stay out of the way, she busied herself in the kitchen.

"Is that a cell phone in your pocket, or are you just happy to see me?" Johnny asked.

Turning, she gave him a small smile. "Your mama said you could show me how to use it."

She pulled the phone out, and Johnny stood very close, showing her the basics. He smelled really good, and she had to stop herself from asking about his cologne.

"Just play with it, call your cousin. Reach out and text someone." He tapped the bill of her cap. "We're about to roll. See you tonight."

"Okay. Have fun." She gripped the phone with both hands, since her palms had gone all wet.

Lacy damn near skipped to her cottage, where she sat on the porch and lit a cigarette. Mrs. Baker told her she could have the rest of the day off, but to be prepared to feed an army in the morning. Staring at her new phone, she wished she had someone to text.

She went back to the main house to borrow the computer. When she checked her bank account, her heart nearly stopped. The payroll deposit was way more than she'd expected. It had to be a mistake. She called Mrs. Baker's cell phone.

"No, honey, it's not a mistake. That's your salary. I'm sure I told you about it the day you interviewed."

"No, ma'am. But that day was a little hectic. I just want to clarify with the room and board, the credit card for household supplies, the medical insurance and everything, you're still paying me that much?"

"Yes, Lacy. Listen, you're practically on call twenty-four, seven. You're up early and to bed late most days. You've got your hands full with Southland, and we like you and want you to stay. We hope your compensation reflects that. Now, go shopping like you planned. Enjoy your day."

"Okay. Go Dawgs. Sic 'em." Lacy repeated the phrases Nick had taught her.

Mrs. Baker was woofing when she hung up.

***

Before midnight, Lacy turned off her bedside lamp. Just as she drifted to sleep, her cell phone rang. She picked it up to see a picture of Johnny with crossed eyes and tongue hanging out. After pressing the answer button, she had to hold it away from her ear because of the loud noise on the other end.

"Johnny, is this a butt dial? I've heard of that, ya know?"

"I need you, Lacy. Can you come get me?" His voice sounded slightly muffled.

She sat up. "Where are you?"

"At a party in town. I'm too drunk to drive and if I pass out… well, right now my buddy, Charlie, is getting a manicure. He's also wearing lipstick. Come save me. Please."

She reached for a notepad and pen. "Give me directions."

After slipping into jeans and a sweatshirt, she put the Georgia hat back on to hide her smashed tangle of curls. She fired Bessie up and set out on a rescue mission. As she drove, she wondered why Johnny had called her, instead of one of his siblings who were staying at the main house. She supposed that was what Mrs. Baker meant about her being on call.

Cars were parked along the street, and Lacy had to pass the house and turn around. It was easier to find a place to park from the other side anyway. She went to the door and knocked.

Max, the mechanic, opened it. "Hey, cutie-pie. Welcome to the party." He staggered toward her and slung a heavy arm around her shoulders, pulling her inside.

She ducked away. "Is Johnny here?"

"Johnny's my bud and a barrel of laughs. Get it? Barrel?" He put both arms out front to indicate a large belly.

Max suffered from the opposite affliction. He was built like a toothpick, and his pants were falling down so his underwear showed. His style wasn't doing a thing for Lacy. She didn't think it was a good look for a greasy haired Southern boy, but he was trying to pull it off.

Lacy felt insulted on Johnny's behalf. She would've never called him fat. He was big and tall, and while he could stand to lose a few pounds, he wouldn't be Johnny if he lost too much.

"Come meet some people." Max pulled her arm.

He led her into the living room, where she saw

a man with a beard passed out on the couch, sporting blue eye shadow and red lipstick.

"There's my ride." Johnny was sitting in a recliner with a young woman on his lap.

Lacy tightened her lips and crossed her arms. Why did it bother her to see him with someone else? She shook it off, as Johnny stood and basically dumped the lady off his legs.

"Don't leave me, Johnny." The girl pouted and grabbed for his arm but missed.

He strode purposefully over to Lacy. "Let's get out of here."

"Wait a minute." Max gripped her arm harder.

It was getting uncomfortable, too much like old times she would rather forget and never revisit.

"Gotta go, Max. See ya later." She tried to tug free and follow Johnny who was almost out the door, but Max yanked her.

As she stumbled, her chin hit his shoulder, causing her teeth to snap shut. The metallic taste of blood filled her mouth before her tongue started to swell. She clutched her jaw with her free hand.

"Ow, are you okay?" Max asked. "If you wanted a hug all you had to do was ask." He pressed his body into her, and she leaned away from him.

"Lacy," Johnny called from the door. "Come on."

Max let her go, and she went outside, not saying goodbye to Max or any of the other drunken party-goers who were staring. When she was surrounded by the shadows of the night, she wiggled her sore jaw and wiped a stray tear. She hated drunks.

She slid behind the wheel of her car, and Johnny crammed his large body into the small space, scooting his seat back as far as it would go.

"Are you pissed I woke you up?" he asked.

"No." She held her jaw in between shifting gears.

"Then what's wrong with you?" He sounded pissy his own self.

"I bit my tongue."

"Oh. I hate when that happens." He took off his cap and hooked it on his knee. "I think Max likes you."

She didn't respond at first. She didn't want to badmouth his friend, and she was grateful he'd fixed her car, but Max was the next to last man she would ever date now. The last was her ex, Stan.

"Not interested."

"What kind of man interests you, Lacy?"

One that doesn't beat me. She shrugged. "It kinda hurts to talk. Sorry."

"You want me to kiss it better?" He wriggled his eyebrows.

She let go of her face to shift gears. "No, but thanks for the offer."

"My lips are available to you anytime." He leaned his head against the seat.

Cutting her eyes his way, she decided to ignore him. He was drunk or else he wouldn't be talking that way. A moment later, a light snore made her look over at his dozing form.

Her eyes fell on his slightly parted lips. Nice lips, which she wanted no part of. Maybe if she kept convincing herself she wasn't interested, she wouldn't think of what kissing him would be like.

Her mouth continued to throb, distracting her from thinking about kissing anyone.

At Southland, she parked and Johnny thanked her before he lumbered off to his cabin.

Before she went to bed, she took two aspirin and prayed her jaw would be better by morning. Having medical insurance for the first time in her life was comforting, but she hated doctor's offices and hospitals and would only go if she had no other choice.

Chapter Nine

Johnny awoke with his head pounding. When would he learn he was too damn old for the party scene? He needed to quit drinking altogether, but after Georgia's big win, he'd wanted to celebrate.

He and a few like-minded friends had pitched in for a keg. The problem with keg parties in their little town was the high schoolers started showing up about the time the old guys were ready to call it a night. He'd held out as long as he could before calling Lacy.

Her showing up was part of his plan to get the college girl off his lap. At least, she'd claimed to be in college, but he doubted it. She'd been rubbing on him for an hour, and it had gotten harder to resist with each passing moment. He hadn't counted on Max trying to woo Lacy the minute she walked in the door. Jealousy had jabbed him with its hairy, green fist, but even drunk, he knew better than to let anyone know it.

He'd toyed with the idea of telling his friends Lacy was his girlfriend—a game similar to the one his brother had played which helped him get his wife—but he didn't think Lacy would play. In the short time he'd known her, he'd learned she could be honest without oversharing. Lying wasn't something he wanted to ask her to do anyway. It wasn't right.

After a long shower, he dragged himself to the main house to join his family for breakfast. The counter looked like a buffet, and Lacy was pouring juice and chocolate milk for the kids. He couldn't face her, so he pulled Carly's pigtails and got giggles and a hug from her.

"Johnny, I meant to tell you yesterday, but you look like you've lost weight," Katie said.

"Yeah. Little Bit over there won't let us have seconds. We eat healthy now." He sniffed the air. "Do I smell bacon?"

"I've lost three pounds," Mama D said. "Now if I could just start exercising regularly, I'd be all right."

"When I first saw Lacy," Paul said, "I remembered a sign hanging in my mother-in-law's kitchen. It says 'Don't trust a skinny cook', but this breakfast is delicious. There are healthy and not so healthy choices." He grinned like a Cheshire cat. "With Aunt May, we only had the one option."

"Dan's pants are big in the waist," Mama D said. "If we keep this up, we'll have to hire a seamstress or buy new clothes."

"Lacy, I hope you can sew because Big Daddy hates to shop for clothes," Katie said.

Johnny looked to Lacy who smiled but didn't say anything. He started paying attention, since it wasn't like her to ignore comments directed at her. Every once in a while, she rubbed her jaw like she might be in pain, though she kept a small smile on her lips.

"Well, Miss Lacy. Can you sew?" Jenny asked her.

"Yeah." Lacy nodded. "I used to make my own clothes."

"Good, 'cause you suck at muddin'," Johnny said.

Everyone laughed, and Lacy's smile widened as her cheeks flushed.

Probably, he shouldn't pick on her in front of everyone. It might embarrass her and may cause speculation. Of course, if he didn't taunt her, they'd notice that too.

Damned if I do and damned if I don't.

He thrummed his fingertips on the counter. All of the speculation was making him speculative. A cigarette would take the edge off, so he went outside.

A couple minutes passed before the door opened and Lacy joined him on the back porch. He passed her the pack of cigarettes, and she took one. He struck his lighter, and she leaned closer to light up.

"Thanks." She exhaled a cloud of smoke.

"Is this your new uniform?" He gestured to her polo, khaki, sneaker combo.

"Why? Do you like it?"

He meant to tease her, but he actually did like

it and told her so.

"I'm saving up for a monogramming machine, and when I get it, I can put an *S* right here," she pointed to the spot above her left breast, "for Southland, ya know?"

"Why would you want to do that?" Again, he was trying to joke with her.

She shrugged and rubbed under her chin. "Seemed like a good idea."

"Your tongue still hurt?"

"It's more my jaw, but yeah."

Johnny's cell rang, and he checked to see Tiffany's name on the screen. He snarled as he answered.

"What time are you coming to get Nick?" she asked.

"I thought we said five."

"I have someplace to be later. Why don't you come get him sooner? And who the hell's Lacy?" Her words tumbled over each other.

He cut his eyes to the woman next to him, and he took one last drag from his cigarette. "I can leave in a minute." He stubbed the cherry out on the sole of his boot. "Lacy's the new housekeeper at Southland."

"You tell that old hag to quit talking smack about me to my son. He told me I was selfish and that word came from Miss Lacy."

"You *are* selfish, Tiffany. Nick didn't need Lacy to tell him that. He knows when he's not wanted."

"I can put up with you talking trash about me in front of him, but I won't put up with the hired help doing it. You get me." Her voice sounded like she was speaking through clenched teeth.

"Tiff, I'm sorry I've said negative things about you in front of Nick. I won't do it anymore. You have my word."

Silence filled the line for a long moment. "Well, thanks. I guess."

He hung up and looked at Lacy. "I'm off to get the boy. You wanna ride to Atlanta?"

"No, I have to mind the kitchen. I better get back in there." Lacy stabbed her thumb toward the back door.

"She thinks you're an old hag." Johnny laughed. "I'd love to see the look on her face the first time she meets you."

Lacy paused at the back door. "I hope that never happens."

"For your sake, I hope so too."

***

Johnny followed his child into the cabin he'd claimed for them after Aunt May and Uncle Ben Hill moved out. "Are you up for movie night, Nick-Nock?"

"Yes, sir. But we have to get Miss Lacy. She promised to watch with us, but it can't be a scary movie."

Johnny sent her a text, and a few minutes later, she showed up with the popcorn.

"How do you feel about *Star Wars*?" he asked. "We're trying to decide on Halloween costumes, and I'm pushing for a Star Wars theme."

"Watch it we will." Her Yoda impersonation wasn't too bad.

When the movie ended, Nick said, “Miss Lacy, you could be Princess Leia.”

“I might make a better Yoda.” She ruffled his hair.

“And Daddy can be Chewbacca.” Nick giggled.

“Are you saying I’m big and hairy?” He tickled Nick who scrambled over to Lacy’s lap. “I can be Darth Vader, and you can be Luke. I’ll walk around all night and tell you I’m your father.” He cupped his hand over his mouth and made a heavy breathing noise.

“There are a lot of characters to choose from,” she said, “especially if you add the other movies. You’ll have Obi-Wan, Lando, Boba Fett, Jabba the Hut, the Ewoks…”

“There aren’t many female characters though. My sisters and nieces will protest.” Johnny crossed his arms over his chest.

“Well, Padmé has a hundred different hairstyles. Leia has several and a few wardrobe choices, one in particular.” Her eyeballs rolled high and glided from side to side. “The droids and Stormtroopers are unisex.”

“What wardrobe choice in particular?” Johnny smirked, knowing full well.

“You said sex.” Nick grinned.

Lacy twisted her lips and spoke out of the side of her mouth. “You know, when she was Jabba’s prisoner.” She turned to Nick. “I said unisex, which means it can be a boy or a girl.”

“Ah, the gold bikini,” Johnny said.

“I remember that part.” Nick bounced on her

lap.

"Every man remembers that part, son." Not wanting to get into a discussion about sex, Johnny changed the subject. "Can you imagine Sara Ann as R2-D2?"

Nick giggled, and the little hollow inside Johnny's chest begin to fill with gratitude for Lacy—and possibly something more. Her ideas were good ones, and if she could sew really well, they'd all look great in time for the party.

Johnny wondered if there was anything she couldn't do, other than stay out of ditches.

Chapter Ten

Lacy got up the next morning with a raging toothache. It was on the same side where her jaw had been bothering her, and she wondered if she'd bitten down on a popcorn kernel the wrong way.

Popping the top off the aspirin bottle, she found only one left. She'd forgotten to pick up extra when she was out on Saturday, but she hadn't expected to need so many. She took the one she had before she made her way to the main house, trying to figure out how to ask Mrs. Baker if she had some without drawing attention to her problem.

Once Lacy had set breakfast on the table, Mrs. Baker came into the kitchen. "Good morning, Lacy."

"Good morning." She hesitated. "Um, do you have some aspirin? And could I have one until I get to the store?" Her tooth ached so badly it hurt to talk.

"I have ibuprofen. Look at me."

Lacy did and Mrs. Baker put her hands on Lacy's cheeks and then felt her forehead. "You have swelling over here in your jaw, and you're feverish. Is it a tooth?"

Nodding, Lacy swallowed. "Feels like it."

"It's your lucky day. I have an appointment this morning to get a filling, but I'll call and tell them to give it to you."

Lucky day, my hindquarters.

Lacy took a step back. "No, that's okay. It'll probably go away."

"Honey, listen to me. If it's infected, you need antibiotics. Dental infections have been known to spread to the brain and cause all sorts of problems, including death."

Lacy's heart kicked up a notch. A brain infection sounded scary, but seeing a dentist ranked just below it.

Mrs. Baker insisted and drove Lacy to Atlanta. As it turned out, the dentist was Dr. Larry Jensen, Mrs. Baker's brother, and part of Lacy's benefits package was free dental treatment with him.

While Mrs. Baker went to see her brother, Lacy filled out the paperwork in the waiting area. A few minutes later, Mrs. Baker opened the door next to the reception desk. "Lacy, you can come on back."

Lacy followed her to a beige room with a beige dental chair and a mix of metal and beige equipment. Neutral colors no longer seemed calming. In her mind, hell wasn't a dark place with orange flames casting eerie shadows. Instead, Lacy felt certain it had khaki dressed walls, sand shaded trim, and mother of pearl floors—exactly like Dr.

Jensen's office.

"Larry says 'It's a Monday', so I'm going to help out by taking the x-rays," Mrs. Baker said. "I used to work as his assistant after my first husband passed away."

"Really?"

She nodded. "I would work the night shift at the hospital, then go home to get the girls ready for school. Afterward, I'd come work here until lunchtime then go home to pass out for a few hours before the girls got off the bus."

"Talk about burning the candle at both ends." Lacy rubbed her damp palms on her pants.

"It was tough. But I had my babies to take care of, don't cha know?" She winked. "When I met Dan, he offered me a job, which paid well enough I could let go of the others."

"Yeah, Dixie." A man walked around the chair. "But I think you worked as many hours launching that home health care service as you did working two jobs." He redirected his attention. "Hi Lacy, I'm Larry, Dixie's older, but better looking, brother."

Lacy shook his hand before he turned to the sink to wash up.

"Here's the periapical x-ray, and the pan is on the other screen," Mrs. Baker said, gesturing to the computer monitor.

"There's a little infection, but I don't see any decay." Dr. Larry put on a pair of blue gloves. "Let me take a look."

Gripping the chair handles, Lacy opened her mouth.

After he poked around a minute, he said, "Cracked tooth. Any idea how it happened?"

She shrugged. "Maybe a popcorn kernel?"

"Several of your teeth have craze lines and a few chips here and there. Is anything rough or sharp?"

Her lungs constricted, making it hard to breathe. She shook her head.

"We'll need to pull it. We could try heroics to save it, like a root canal and crown, but chances are it'll fail and you'll lose it anyway. It's a wisdom tooth—your only one."

"Just pull it," she said. "It wasn't working anyway."

"Funny." He grinned.

Mrs. Baker set things out on a tray, and Lacy spotted something that looked like a needle. A cold sweat broke out all over her body, and her vision narrowed.

"Are you nervous?" He patted her shoulder. "Would you like a little gas to help relax?"

She nodded. They put a gas mask over her nose, and a couple moments later, he gave her a shot in the cheek. It didn't hurt as bad as she'd expected, so she loosened her grip, flaring and flexing her fingers.

"All right, we're gonna let you sit and get numb for a few minutes. Keep breathing through your nose, and Dixie will be right here if you need anything."

Closing her eyes, Lacy concentrated on inhaling the happy gas. It actually worked, and she heard herself sigh.

Unsure how much time had passed, Lacy blinked when she heard Dr. Larry's voice again. She opened, and he probed around her tooth to see if she could feel it.

Nothing. This would be no big deal.

He had a tool, which looked like a flat-head screwdriver he used to nudge her tooth. Then Mrs. Baker passed him a pair of pliers with which he pushed one direction, then the other. Pain shot through her jaw, so she held her breath and pressed her head into the chair to keep from jerking away.

Lacy didn't realize she was crying until Mrs. Baker wiped her face with little squares of cotton.

Dr. Larry put the pliers down. "Where does it hurt?"

Lacy's chest heaved, and she sniffled a minute before she pointed to her jaw on the other side. He looked at the computer. From the corner of her eye, she could see her x-ray on the screen. It turned colors and different shades of gray, black, and white as he examined it.

"Have you ever had your jaw broken, Lacy?"

She nodded and sniffed again, trying to get some air in her lungs.

"How long ago?"

"Three and a half years." She swiped at her eyes, but bumped the plastic thing on her nose instead.

"Boyfriend?" he asked.

Making a point not to look at Mrs. Baker, Lacy dipped her chin once.

"I'm going to turn up the nitrous. Breathe through your nose. I want to try one more time, but if it's too painful, I'll stop and send you to a friend of mine. He's an oral surgeon, and he can put you to sleep, so when you wake up, it'll be done. Does that sound like a plan?"

She tried to smile, and he patted her arm. Mrs. Baker wiped her tears, including the ones puddled in her ears.

On the second try, the tooth came out. They told her to bite on some cotton and breathe the oxygen.

She couldn't because she broke down and cried uncontrollably. The chair back rose up, and Mrs. Baker hugged her hard. Lacy hadn't been held in so long, all she could do was cling to her employer and sob.

When she quieted down, Dr. Larry patted her back. "Here are prescriptions for antibiotics and something for pain, just in case. Get some rest. No smoking. No drinking through a straw."

"Th-thank you," Lacy said around the gauze in her mouth.

"No problem at all." He looked at his sister. "Call me if she needs anything."

Once in the car, Mrs. Baker touched her hand. "Let's get your scripts filled, then get you home so you can lay down."

It sounded good, but Lacy had chores to do. Maybe if she took a pain pill, she'd be okay to work when the bleeding stopped.

"My first husband hit me once," Mrs. Baker said.

Lacy didn't say anything because she was still biting on a cotton pad, but she almost laughed. She wished she'd only been hit once.

"I was pregnant with Katie. The warning signs were there—the escalating violence. It started with yelling, then throwing things at me. When he hit me, I packed a bag and took Liz to my sister's house. He came and begged for forgiveness—begged me to go home to him." Mrs. Baker's eyes were fixed on the road.

"He was an alcoholic, so I told him he had one chance. If he ever struck me or the kids, I'd leave for good. I told him not to come home drunk again either. He didn't, which is why the girls think he was an absentee dad. I'd rather them think that than to see him drunk and violent."

Lacy pulled a soggy wad of cotton out of her mouth and put it in a little plastic sack. "It's good he heeded your warnings. And good that Mr. Baker is such a nice guy."

"Dan's the best man. And his boys are just like him. None of them would raise a hand against a woman." She smirked. "Except for maybe Danny when he fights with his wife."

"What?" Lacy heard the alarm in her own voice as she was about to stuff more gauze in the hole where her tooth used to be.

Mrs. Baker laughed. "They're combat trained. Jane was a police officer and they… What's the word? Spar? You know? Practice fighting—like karate or kickboxing or something."

With her mouth full, Lacy shifted her chin side to side. "Oh."

Mrs. Baker took Lacy to the pharmacy, where she got her prescriptions filled and picked up a bottle of ibuprofen.

By the time they returned to Southland, it was early afternoon.

Johnny met them on the porch. "Where's my lunch, woman? I'm starving."

"Make yourself a sandwich, Johnny," Mrs. Baker said.

"I'll do it." Lacy went into the kitchen, poking her cheek with her finger because it was starting to wake up.

"You should rest for a little while, Lacy. Johnny can make his own lunch."

"What's wrong?" Johnny asked.

"Nothing." Mrs. Baker gave her a gentle push out the door. "Take the cart. I'll come check on you after a while."

***

Johnny waited until Lacy was out of sight. "Is she okay?"

"She'll be fine. Just had a rough day." Mama D pulled the tea pitcher out of the fridge.

Johnny held the door open. "Is she sick?"

"I really shouldn't say anything, but she had a broken tooth. Thinks it might've been a popcorn kernel."

"We had popcorn last night while we watched a movie." He grabbed turkey, lettuce, and mustard.

"Johnny, you aren't making a move on her, are you?" She tilted her head to one side, eyes narrowed.

"No, ma'am. Nick invited her." He unwound the bread tie.

Mama D looked up at the ceiling. "Last night

wouldn't have been enough time for it to get infected that much. It had to have cracked sooner."

"She said she bit her tongue Saturday night." He put his sandwich together.

"That could've been it." Mama D left him to eat alone.

Later, he found it hard to concentrate on getting the old Massey-Ferguson tractor running because he couldn't stop thinking about Lacy.

When she came in to make dinner, Johnny looked at her closely. "What were you doing when you bit your tongue the other night?"

She met his eyes briefly, then turned away. "I don't remember."

"Liar." He stood on the other side of the bar, his heart thumping hard. Why wouldn't she tell him the truth?

"What makes you think I'm lying?" Her hand rested on her hip.

"Because you twisted your lips and didn't look at me when you answered."

"Are you a body language expert or something?" She spoke with her mouth nearly closed.

"Quit trying to change the subject. Why don't you want to tell me?"

"Because it might make you mad, and it was an accident, and there's nothing you can do about it." She still wouldn't look at him.

He moved until he stood right in front of her. "Tell me anyway."

"I don't want to."

"Why not?" Johnny clenched his fists.

She backed away. “Don’t yell at me. It’s none of your business.”

“What’s going on?” Mama D looked from him to Lacy. “Johnny, I told you she wasn’t feeling well. Leave her alone.”

“She won’t tell me how she bit her tongue.”

Mama D’s eyes narrowed. “Leave it alone, Johnny.”

“Her not telling me makes me think the worst.”

“It was an accident…sort of,” Lacy said. “I feel kind of stupid. My chin ran into someone’s shoulder.”

“Whose shoulder?”

Lacy closed her eyes and dropped her head. “Your friend Max. You were right there when it happened.”

Johnny clamped his teeth together, so he wouldn’t cuss as fury sparked in his core. He thought back to that night, trying to remember. When he had stepped back in the house, Max had Lacy by the arm, and she’d looked frightened. She’d been holding her jaw.

“Johnny,” Mama D said. “Go see about Nick.”

“Nick’s fine.” He lightly gripped Lacy’s upper arms. “If anyone ever hurts you, or even scares you a little, I want you to tell me. Okay?”

She looked up at him with wide eyes. “Why?”

“So I can kick their—”

“Johnny—” Mama D interrupted.

“Dad,” Nick ran in the back door. “Hey, Miss Lacy.”

Johnny turned around and picked Nick up to hug him. “Did you get your homework finished?”

"Yes, sir. Guess what, Miss Lacy? I'm getting my green belt in karate tomorrow."

"Awesome." She high-fived him. "Maybe you can teach me some moves." Straightening her fingers, she made little chopping motions with her hands.

"You should come. I mean, I think they let grown-ups take lessons too. Don't they, Dad?"

"Son, that's a great idea. What do you say, Miss Lacy? They have kickboxing for adults right after Nick's class. I was thinking of trying it out so Uncle Danny and Aunt Jane can't whip me."

"That's a good idea, Lacy," Mama D said. "If you're interested. Although tomorrow might be too soon to start. You should take another day to heal. You could go watch the class though to see if you think you might like it."

It was a little odd for Mama D to also encourage Lacy to take martial arts. He squinted his eyes at his mom. She knew something.

"Um, I'll think about it." Lacy opened the refrigerator.

"Nick, go practice your guitar until dinner's ready." He put his son down.

"Yes, sir." Nick ran to the other room.

Lacy's back was to him, and he was about to say something when Mama D got his attention by making a slashing motion across her throat.

Johnny threw his hands up and followed Nick. A moment later, Mama D joined them in the recreation room. They listened to Nick play and sing a song, applauding when he finished. When he started another one, Mama D cleared her throat.

"There're some things I can't tell you." Mama D spoke softly. "But trust me when I say, don't bully her. Ever."

What? He was the anti-bully and everyone knew it.

And he could think of few things worse than a secret he wasn't privy to. It would drive him crazy. "And the kickboxing?"

"Johnny, sweetie, have your sisters' experiences taught you nothing? It's not exactly the same, but every woman should know how to defend herself."

He nodded because without saying much at all, Mama D had just told him what he'd wondered about Lacy.

Once upon a time, she'd been somebody's punching bag, and Johnny aimed to see it never happened again.

Chapter Eleven

Nearly a month had passed and Lacy had almost finished the costumes for the Halloween party. She kept imagining how much fun it would be to dress up and give out candy to the kids.

In the meantime, Johnny and Nick had been dragging her to kickboxing twice a week, and she'd had to give up smoking for real. Her lungs couldn't handle the cardiovascular workout she endured. The instructor had taken her aside to work on her technique and had taught her some basic self-defense in the process. She'd never felt empowered before, but taking out her pent up frustration on a sack of sand was doing it for her.

Humming, she scrubbed the sink in Johnny's cottage with extra vigor and thought of Nick. He'd been practicing his guitar more because he wanted to play for his Aunt Lizabelle when she came for the party.

One day, not thinking, Lacy had started singing

along and Nick went crazy. He wanted her to sing more, but she told him she would only do it if he kept it their secret. She thought she sounded good in the car and in the shower, but she didn't need anyone telling her different like Stan used to do. So now, she only sang for herself…and Nick.

When they were alone in the house while Nick practiced, she'd play along on his drum set. She had no idea what she was doing, but it was fun to pretend she was a rock star for a few minutes. Nick told her she was a natural, but she suspected he was just being nice. It was cathartic to bang on the drums, almost as good as punching a bag—a much needed release.

She was having a rock star moment, playing air drums, as she bent over the bathtub.

"What are you doing?"

She jumped, shrieked, and turned to see Johnny standing in the doorway, shirtless.

He laughed as she tried to regain her composure and not stare at his chest. She'd never seen it before, and her eyes were drawn to all his smooth skin lightly dusted with dark hair.

Lord-a-mercy.

She wanted to look again and had to force her head back over the side of the tub. "I'm working. What are *you* doing?"

"A cloud came up, and I got soaked. I need to change into dry clothes."

"Okay, let me just rinse, and I'll give you some privacy."

"No worries. Just stay in here a minute." He closed the bathroom door, leaving her on her knees and sweating inside her sexy yellow rubber gloves.

She wouldn't be able to get the image of his massive chest out of her head. In kickboxing class, he normally wore sleeveless shirts, so she'd seen his arm muscles. He picked up feed sacks like they weighed nothing at all, showcasing his strength. But his chest…he didn't even need six-pack abs to improve the view.

Whew! She'd gotten herself hot and bothered just by picturing one of her bosses half-naked.

She wiped the sweat from her forehead with the bend of her elbow, which was also damp with perspiration.

It had been a while since she'd had a boyfriend, but she reminded herself she was out of the man business…forever. She attracted the worst kind of men, and she couldn't be trusted to make a good choice. The single life wasn't so bad.

When she began to rinse the cleanser away, the door opened. Johnny stood there, buttoning his shirt. She got another glimpse of *the chest,* it was a reality unto itself, like art, and need curled low in her belly. Closing her eyes, she turned away.

"You okay?"

"Yep, fine as wine." She swallowed hard. "I just have to do the floors, and I'll be out of your hair." Her heart flitted around in her chest, like a damn butterfly.

"Lacy, you're not bothering me." He was quiet a moment. "Am I bothering you?"

She rolled her eyes and shook her head as she picked up the cleaning caddy. Her attempt to squeeze past him out of the bathroom only brought her eye level with the body part she wanted to rest her head on…and maybe kiss.

Stop being a pervert, Lacy.

He lounged in the doorway, grinning down at her. Too late, she realized she'd twisted her mouth. It was one of her tells, and Johnny had picked up on it a long time ago. He was gonna call her on it, and she didn't know what to say.

I think you're handsome and sweet, and I want to curl up in your lap in front of a fire.

"How are the costumes coming along?" He tucked his shirt into his jeans.

"Good." Relief caused her shoulders to droop. "I'm almost finished. Did you get the helmets and plastic weapons?"

He cinched his belt tighter because his pants were too big in the waist. "Yeah. Wanna see?"

With the giddiness of an eight-year-old, she nodded.

He opened the closet and pulled out a big cardboard box. He put on the Darth Vader helmet and pressed a button to make the breathing noise.

She laughed. "You might scare the kids."

Picking up a white Stormtrooper helmet, he handed it to her.

She pulled it down over her face, and it was his turn to laugh. Since almost every female in the family wanted to be Leia or Padmé, Lacy had decided to be a Stormtrooper. With her unisex build, it suited her, and she could hide behind the mask.

Johnny gave her a toy blaster gun, which made the high-pitched whirring noise, just like in the movie, and he took one of the lightsabers. She pretended to blast him, while he tapped her lightly on the arm with the plastic sword.

She laughed so hard she had to sit down and catch her breath, partly lifting the face cover. "Nick's going to love this."

Johnny rested his helmet on top of his head. "Are you ready to meet the rest of the family on Thursday?"

"I guess so. I'm glad I'll be wearing this at the party." She tapped the mask.

He lifted the hard plastic until her face was fully exposed and leaned in, his breath hot against her cheek. "They're gonna love you, just like everyone else."

***

Johnny had been working hard to get ready for the party. With a parched mouth, he headed to the main house for a drink. The Bakers always held their big party the weekend before Halloween, and his older brother and sister would be there soon, so he'd gotten an early start on the chores.

Before he went inside, he kicked his boots off at the back door, not wanting to ruin Lacy's clean floors. He walked straight to the fridge and stopped short when he heard music. He followed his ears and peeked around the corner to see Nick playing guitar and Lacy next to him, singing.

Lacy was a beautiful woman, but her voice put her in a different stratosphere. Since he could play almost any stringed instrument, he had a pretty good ear for music. The sound floating on the air from her mouth put him in a trance. His pants grew tight, and he turned away to adjust.

He'd been fighting a growing attraction to her since the day they'd met, but… How had he not known this about her?

When he thought about it, her speaking voice gave her away. She had such a smooth, clear tone.

Retreating to the kitchen with his mouth dryer than before, he chugged a huge glass of water. He knew without being told Lacy wouldn't want anyone to hear her sing. As he walked back to his cabin, he acknowledged he was a little jealous of his son.

He needed to get his mind off of her. It had been too long since he'd been out with a woman. His last girlfriend had threatened to kill him, literally, so it was an understatement to say he was a little gun-shy. Another colossal fail in a long line of being attracted to the wrong women.

Chapter Twelve

Lacy had roasting pans ready to go in the ovens when Nick ran from the front room to the back door. “They’re here. They’re here.”

Johnny and Mr. and Mrs. Baker were right behind him. Lacy stayed in the kitchen. Even though they treated her like she was one of them, she wasn’t part of their family. She had to constantly remind herself to stay out of their business. Already, she’d caused a little trouble for Nick and Johnny with Tiffany.

People filed into the house. Johnny had a baby in his arms, as did Mr. and Mrs. Baker. The little boy Mr. Baker carried was older than the others. He held a Spiderman toy in one hand and pointed to the refrigerator.

“He’s thirsty, Big Daddy,” Liz said.

Lacy recognized her from pictures and liked her nickname, Lizabelle. She looked like Maddie, but taller, and Mrs. Baker, but younger.

"What's he allowed to drink?" Lacy asked, opening the fridge door.

"You must be Lacy. It's so nice to meet you." Liz hugged her, and Lacy blinked in surprise. "Water's fine. Let me get his sippy cup. This is Ethan by the way."

"Hi, Ethan." Lacy waved her fingers at the child.

"Wink?" His little voice was the sweetest.

"Yeah, buddy. We're gonna get you a drink," she said.

"Lacy, this is my oldest son Danny and his wife Jane," Mr. Baker said.

"Nice to meet you." She shook their hands and tried not to wince at Jane's strong grip. It matched the rest of her, since she was a buff-looking woman.

They told her the twins' names, but they were only ten months old, so Lacy wouldn't be having any real conversations with them.

"Lacy, do you need any help to get ready for the party?" Jane asked.

"Um, I still have to make a few snacks and appetizers." Lacy shifted her weight from foot to foot. "I thought I'd let the older kids help me tomorrow night when everyone's here. We're gonna make ghosts and witches hats and a whole bunch of stuff I found in Mrs. Baker's magazines."

"Speaking of magazines," Johnny said. "I found a *Men's Health* in my cottage. I think somebody wants me to trade my two liter in for a six-pack."

"You look great, brother. I hardly recognized you." Liz put her arm around him. "How much weight have you lost?"

"About twenty-five pounds. I've been telling y'all Little Bit ain't feeding us nothing. She's the food police."

Lacy turned to fill Ethan's sippy cup with water and to hide her smile.

"I've lost ten pounds, and your daddy's lost fifteen." Mrs. Baker put an arm around Lacy. "She's made a huge difference in our eating habits. Haven't you, honey?"

Lacy's cheeks warmed. "I guess so."

***

The next night after dinner, Lacy started making the ghost cookie treats with a couple of the kids, while the Bakers gathered with more instruments than she'd ever seen. They were part Partridge Family, part Lynyrd Skynyrd.

Nick played his songs and received appropriate praise from his favorite aunt. Lacy cheered from the kitchen.

Holding a baby in each arm, Johnny approached. "That white chocolate is tickling my nostrils."

"Too bad your hands are full," she teased.

"Don't you want to hold one of these little bundles of joy, so I can taste test the merchandise? I need to make sure it's fit to eat."

Lacy picked up a Nutter Butter coated with still wet white chocolate and put it in Johnny's mouth. His lips caught the tips of her fingers as they closed, and the moan which came from him made her girl parts as warm as the melted chocolate.

She wiped her hands on her apron and held her

arms out. "Give me that precious little girl. Dillon, isn't it?"

Johnny nodded and passed her the baby and then with his newly freed hand, he snatched another ghost.

"Oh, my God," he said around a mouthful. "This is so good. You should've never let me taste it. I won't be able to stop."

He reached for another, and she smacked his hand, causing the baby to laugh. "Remember to chew slowly and savor every bite. You don't get thirds."

"Aw, come on. It's Halloween."

She smiled at his pleading tone and almost relented and let him have another one, but she was saved by the big brother.

"Johnny, aren't you going to show off your mad guitar skills?" Danny took the baby boy from Johnny's arms and sent him to join the family jam session.

"I bet Johnny plays for you all the time," Danny said. "Can I try one of these?"

She bounced the baby on her hip. "Yes. I mean, no."

Danny paused with a ghost halfway to his mouth.

"No, I've never hear Johnny play, and yes, you can have one." She held up a finger to indicate the number one.

If everyone snuck over to try a ghost, she'd have to go back to the store. Instead of Ghost Busters, she was Nutter Butter Busters.

"God, this is tasty." Danny chewed. "I can't

believe Johnny hasn't played for you. He's really good."

"Nick plays for me." She rocked side to side and smiled at the baby in her arms.

"He's getting good, too. I'm impressed." Danny held his finger, still coated with white chocolate, to his son's lips. The baby sucked it like a pacifier.

"My brother seems different. And I don't mean the weight loss." There was the undertone of a question in his words.

Lacy shrugged. If Danny wanted to ask her something, he was gonna have to come out and say it. She wasn't into guessing games.

"Do you play or sing?"

Twisting her lips, she shook her head before using her free hand to put mini chocolate chips on the ghosts to give them eyes.

"Just a quick heads up," Danny said. "Tell no one about Liz's son." This time his statement brooked no question at all.

Lacy furrowed her brow and studied him. "Okay."

"The baby's father doesn't know about him. He didn't want kids, so Liz made the decision to keep it from him."

"Good for her. More parents should care so much."

Danny raised his eyebrows and was about to speak when Nick rounded the corner.

"I did it, Miss Lacy. I played my songs."

She put her free arm around him. "I know. I heard, and you sounded wonderful, just like always.

I'm so proud of you."

He hugged her waist, and she smoothed his hair.

He spoke in a loud whisper. "Do you want to sing with me?"

"Shh, no silly. That's our secret." She glanced at Danny who pretended not to be listening. "You know I can't sing."

She winked at Nick, and as a distraction, she offered him a ghost.

***

Johnny passed his guitar off to Nick and stepped outside for some fresh air. His cigarette cravings still nagged him, but he was seriously trying to quit.

The night air was a little crisp, which meant it was just right for the Halloween party.

A few minutes later, the back door opened and Lacy came out.

"Finished?" He glided his rocking chair back and forth.

"Finally. My feet are killing me. I'm going to soak in a hot bath."

"You could use the hot tub." He pointed. "It hardly gets used anymore, but Jane normally gets in it when she's here. Says it helps her sore muscles because she runs a hundred miles a day."

"Uh-uh."

"Well, not a hundred, but her and Danny run about five miles a day."

"I only run if I'm being chased, and thankfully, Jake over here doesn't like to chase." She bent to pet the canine's head.

"Jake, nor Jack, likes to walk, much less run. They're the laziest damn dogs I've ever seen."

She chuckled and sat on the steps to rub Jake's sides. Lacy was Jake's favorite human, and if she was outside, he was with her. When the weather was nice, he slept on her little porch. *The suck up.*

"You want me to see if anyone's up for a soak?" Johnny asked because the idea was appealing, and he wanted to pursue it.

"Um, I don't think I'd be comfortable with people in the hot tub." She didn't look at him.

"You wouldn't be comfortable in there by yourself either."

She tilted her head. "How do you know I haven't been sneaking out here at night?"

"Have you?" He arched one eyebrow.

Her mouth twisted. "No."

"I dare you to get in the hot tub."

She smiled. "You actually think that'll work on me?"

"It was worth a shot." He shrugged. "Go on down to your cottage and soak all alone in the bathtub. If you get bored, come back over here. I'm gonna see who I can round up." He stood and stretched his arms over his head.

After staring at him for a long second, she shook her head and walked off into the dark with Jake by her side.

Had he seen heat in her eyes? Couldn't have.

Don't be a dumbass, Shake and Bake. The only thing females find attractive about you is your wallet.

The door opened again. "Hey, brother."

"Lizabelle, how's life?" He gestured to the seat beside him and sat down again.

"Good, just enjoying my little man. How 'bout you?" The rocking chair beside his began to glide forward and back.

He rested his elbows on the wooden arm rests. "Trying to be a better man."

"For who?" The teasing smile in her voice was as clear as the one on her face.

"For myself. For my son. For my future wife." He added the last part because he suspected Liz would if he didn't. The women in his family had something he envied—insane intuition. If he had it, he'd stop picking the wrong women.

Liz smirked. "You met her yet?"

He raised his brows before he shot her a slow wink and looked away.

Chapter Thirteen

Lacy had just gotten out of the bathtub when there was a knock at the door.

"Just a minute." She hurriedly dried off, and because she was still damp, she struggled into her clothes.

When she finally opened the door, Liz stood on the other side, her turquoise eyes full of warmth.

"You weren't in bed, were you?"

"Not yet." Lacy glanced down at her bare feet.

"The kids are going to bed. The adults are getting in the Jacuzzi. I've heard so much about you, and I'd love to get to know you better. Why don't you come join us?" Her tone was sincere.

Thank goodness Lacy had just shaved her legs, but she still didn't want to prance around half-naked in front of people.

She fidgeted with the hem of her well-worn T-shirt. "Um."

Liz touched her arm. "Don't worry about how

you look in a bathing suit. We won't pay any attention. All of us are hiding some physical flaw or another."

None of the Baker women were flawed in any way, as far as Lacy could tell. This was Johnny's doing. He'd sent Liz on this errand. Part of Lacy wanted to refuse and prove a point, but she wasn't a hundred percent sure what her point was.

She did want to get to know the other family members better. Nick spoke so highly of Liz that Lacy felt like she knew her a little already. "Um, okay. I'll be just a minute."

Liz sat on the bench Johnny had placed out in front of her cottage. "I'll wait and walk with you."

Lacy found her tankini shoved in the back of a drawer. Because her ribs poked out and people always commented on it, she didn't like to expose her mid-section.

As they walked toward the main house, Liz said, "Danny told me about your reaction to my baby daddy news." Her mouth hinted at a smile before it faded. "May I ask why you support my decision without knowing the circumstances?"

"Any kid who's ever felt unwanted by their parents would back you up."

"Well, I appreciate it. Nick adores you, and he told me your secret." Liz put her hand on Lacy's shoulder. "I swore I wouldn't tell."

She chuckled. "He's a great kid, but maybe not so good at keeping secrets."

Liz blew out a loud breath. "I worry he might inadvertently tell his mom about Ethan. Tiffany caused me some problems when I was with Ethan's dad, and she's the last person I need to find out."

Lacy nodded. "She and I don't belong to each other's fan clubs."

"Johnny told me she thinks you're old." Liz's chuckle was throaty, the kind a man would find sexy. "She's probably picturing Aunt May who was the quintessential elderly Southern woman."

They approached the pool area where everyone was already sitting chest deep in hot water, waiting on them. Lacy swallowed and forced her feet to keep moving.

"I told you Lizabelle could talk her into it," Mrs. Baker said.

"Are you sure we'll fit?" Lacy asked. "I foresee an overflow when we reach maximum capacity."

"This'll be fun," Paul said. "Like trying to fit twelve adults into a Fiat."

"Or like muddin'," Danny said.

Lacy's face warmed. They *all* knew the mud had gotten the best of her.

"Don't worry, Lacy." Liz squeezed her shoulder. "We've all put that Blazer in a ditch at some point."

"Yeah, but were you stone-cold sober when you did it?" Lacy asked.

Gales of laughter rose into the cool night air.

Liz tugged off her sweat pants, and Lacy followed her lead. She hated taking her clothes off in front of people. She'd never make it as a stripper, and not just because she didn't have the body for the job. The thought made her miss Trina. When they'd cleaned houses together, they'd joked about how much more money they might make as exotic dancers.

Lacy pulled off her sweatshirt and slid into the hot tub between Liz and Johnny, not making eye contact with anyone, especially the man next to her.

***

Johnny kept his eyes fixed on his brother who sat across from him. He only let himself watch Lacy in his peripheral vision. Knowing she would look great in a bathing suit, his mind didn't need any more images to keep him awake at night.

"Is Nick staying in the main house with his cousins?" she asked.

"Yeah. The kids sleep together in the playroom, except for the itty bitty ones. Ethan pitched a fit, and Liz relented and let him sleep with them since Beth and Jenny promised to look after him."

"Johnny, this is the first time you haven't had to give up your cottage for someone," Lizabelle said.

"I'm still willing if anyone wants to arm wrestle me for it." He winked.

"Speaking of arm wrestling," Jane said. "What are you doing to get those guns?"

"Hey, I've got *your* guns right here." Danny wrapped an arm around his wife.

"In addition to haulin' hay and feed, I've been taking a class. Isn't that right, Little Bit?" he elbowed Lacy.

"Right." She nodded once.

Mama D explained about their kickboxing class, which saved Johnny from having to do it.

Once upon a time, he would have bragged about it to his brother. But looking good in his brother's eyes was no longer a priority. He cared more what Nick thought of him and the example he was setting for his son.

"Are you kids gonna ride tomorrow?" Big Daddy asked.

"Heck, yeah," Liz said. "You're riding with us, aren't you?"

"Who's gonna watch my grandbabies?"

"I'll watch them," Lacy volunteered.

"We have to ride early, if I'm going to do all y'all's hair and makeup, ladies," Katie said.

"You don't want to ride with us, Lacy?" Liz asked.

She shook her head.

"Have you ever ridden before?" Paul asked.

"No," she said.

"I haven't ridden much, but it's fun once you get used to it," Jane said.

"That's because she's a city girl, but what's your excuse?" Johnny nudged her.

"Horses weren't allowed in the trailer park where I grew up," she said.

Everyone laughed, except for Johnny. He knew she wasn't joking.

Chapter Fourteen

The next morning after breakfast, almost everyone went to ride horses. Lacy stayed behind with Mrs. Baker, two sleeping babies, and Ethan, who she'd learned was nineteen months old. Mrs. Baker sat at the table, holding Ethan and helping him color a picture of a barn.

Lacy had done most of the preparation for the chili in the days leading up to the party, so she got out three large crock pots. After she'd added all the ingredients, she got the crescent rolls wrapped around the mummy dogs. She wouldn't bake them until closer to the time of the party, but she wanted to have them ready to go in the ovens.

Working at Southland was a cook's dream come true. When she'd first arrived and saw a second refrigerator in the butler's pantry, she didn't think she'd ever use it. Now, it nearly overflowed with party food, and she was grateful Mrs. Baker and Miss May had gotten it. The six-burner industrial stove and double wall ovens made Lacy's life much easier when she was feeding an army like the Bakers.

One of the twins started to cry, so Lacy washed her hands and picked him up.

"You're good with the little ones, Lacy," Mrs. Baker said. "Do you want your own someday?"

"I love kids, but I always swore I'd never have any, unless I could give them a good life." She soothed the baby by hugging him close and patting his butt. He needed a change.

"What's your idea of a good life?"

Lacy laid the baby on a pallet on the floor. "The main things are time and love. You know better than me that if you have to bust your hump working two jobs to make ends meet, it doesn't leave much time left over to give the kids." She reached for the diaper bag. "I'm not judging you, by the way. In fact, I applaud you. You did what you had to do, and you were blessed."

"I agree. I went without sleep many times, so I could go to dance recitals and watch my girls cheer at ballgames. I was lucky my sister and niece helped me so much. Not lucky, *blessed*, like you said." Mrs. Baker smiled. "How did you get so wise?"

"It must've been that wisdom tooth." Lacy laughed. "I guess I watched to see how others did it. My aunt, Trina's mom, she did it right. She's the one who taught me to sew. She was a seamstress and worked from home, so she could be there when Trina got home from school. She raised me more than my own mother."

"You're a very bright young woman, Lacy. In

case I haven't told you, we're so happy you're here. You're a great housekeeper and person. We adore you. Nick especially."

Lacy's heart lifted with the praise. "I adore him…y'all, too."

"I can tell." She sighed. "I just wish Tiffany would cherish Nick as much as you."

Lacy nodded as she fastened a fresh diaper on Davis. "You're also adorable." She picked him up to snuggle and rubbed his fuzzy head. "I love that baby smell."

***

With the party about to begin, Lacy wore her costume with her helmet pushed on top of her head. Nick kept shooting at her with his toy blaster, and she was getting winded from ducking behind furniture.

"You're wearing me out, Nick." She collapsed onto a kitchen chair.

Everyone came down the stairs, dressed and ready. Maddie was the brave soul who'd donned the gold bikini. Heath had convinced her that her store bought boobs would be perfect for the costume, and Lacy agreed they were, wondering how much they cost. Maddie was gorgeous, and the way her equally handsome husband looked at her triggered a longing inside Lacy. Would a man ever look at her with such admiration?

Danny was outfitted as Han Solo and Paul, Luke Skywalker. Mr. Baker was Jabba the Hutt, and Mrs. Baker was Boba Fett. They looked amazing.

Liz and Jane were Leia in white dresses, but Liz had the bun hair and Jane had a long French braid. The twins were dressed as Ewoks and Ethan was Yoda. Katie was a very pretty Obi-Wan and her husband, Robert, played Lando, complete with Billy Dee Williams hair.

Paul's wife, Jen, agreed to be C-3PO, and after Heath put his Chewbacca mask in place, he scared the crap out of Lacy.

Tyler was R2-D2. The girl grandkids were Padmé—all with different hairstyles. The other boys were Stormtroopers, and of course, Johnny was an imposing Darth Vader.

Lacy turned on the movie soundtrack she'd downloaded for the party with Nick's help. It would get old by the night's end, but it pumped everyone up.

Jane set up a fancy camera and tripod for a family photo shoot. Nick dragged Lacy to the little group of Stormtroopers, and they held their blasters.

"Y'all look like miniature Charlie's Angels with those guns," Johnny said.

The kids didn't know what he meant, so Lacy showed them how to strike the pose. They got a good picture with Darth Vader in the middle of his storm troopers, a giant amid small white ants.

By nightfall, when the haunted hayrides took place, there were fifty kids and about as many adults. Lacy laughed when she was introduced to a family friend, Jason, and his wife, Roxanne. He came as a priest, and she was a pregnant nun, seven months along in real life. Their son, who was Nick's age, was dressed as Darth Maul, so he made a great addition to the theme of the party.

"You wanna go on the hayride?" Johnny asked

before he activated the noise maker on his mask. "You can ride with me."

"It's not scary, is it?"

"We have to keep it appropriate for the little kids, but don't worry, I'll keep you safe." He waved his lightsaber in the air.

"Okay then." She followed him out to the tractor, and excitement skittered through her.

Each of the three tractors pulled a wagon filled with hay. Orange lights strung along the sides kept it from being pitch dark.

"We used to use the horses to pull the wagons, but the tractors are easier and they poop less." Johnny climbed up onto the seat of the tractor and reached down for her. With one pull, she practically landed on top of him. He seated her on the fender next to him and waited for Mr. Baker to tell him the passengers were loaded and ready to go.

Lacy loved hearing the chatter of the kids, intoxicated with sugar and trepidation.

Johnny had done as much decorating in the woods as she'd done in the house. Ghosts and mummies hung from the trees. Witches and goblins were in strategic places with spotlights illuminating them.

"This looks really great, Johnny. You done good." She had to lean down to his ear to be heard over the motor, and fear gripped her as she began slipping.

He wrapped an arm around her and pulled her onto his lap. "Whoa, Little Bit, I thought I lost you." He readjusted his hand on the big round steering wheel. "Thanks for the compliment. The house looks great too. Except I keep walking into those fake cobwebs."

"Thanks for not letting me get run over by the tractor. I think I peed a little."

"And now you're in my lap. Great. Just Great." Sarcasm.

It was one of the many things she liked about him.

She shivered, and he pulled her closer to his warm body. Her heart beat harder. Being so close to him enveloped her in a cloud of protection, a place she desired more than she should.

When they got back to the house, she thanked him again and headed straight to the kitchen to make sure enough food and snacks were still available. He followed.

"There you are, Johnny." The woman who said it wore a gold bikini. She didn't look as good as Maddie, but she didn't look bad either.

Lacy kept on task, but observed from the corner of her eye, as the woman ran her hands up and down Johnny's chest.

"What are you doing here, Tiffany?" He took both of her hands in one of his.

The hair on the back of Lacy's neck sprung to attention.

"I was just asking Liz about that kid she's carrying," Tiffany said.

Lacy leapt into action. "He's with me. Thanks for watching him, Liz." Lacy took the little boy. "Oh, it looks like he might need a new diaper."

As Lacy took Ethan upstairs, she heard Tiffany ask who she was.

First, Lacy went to the playroom, but it overflowed with kids. Ethan really could use a new diaper, so she went to the room Liz slept in to find the diaper bag.

Ethan played with her helmet, while she changed his diaper. "You are so precious."

"I thought you'd be older…and fatter," Tiffany said from the doorway. "Whose kid?"

"My cousin," Lacy said. "His mama had to work tonight, and I thought he might like to play with the other kids at the party."

"You're the bitch who's been talking trash about me to my son." Tiffany took a few steps into the room.

"Ah. Little ears. Language," Lacy said, a sweat bead running down her back. "I don't know what Nick said, but I was speaking generally, not specifically."

"Excuse me." Jane stood in the doorway. "We haven't met because well, I'm part of this family and you're not. I've been asked to escort you off of the premises."

"Screw you coming in here telling me I'm not welcome. This ain't your house. My son lives here. I can come and go as I please, and I have business with this scrawny little bitch."

She returned her attention to Lacy and moved closer. Lacy ignored her and bent over Ethan to get her helmet. The next thing she knew, her head was yanked backwards by her ponytail. Even when Stan used to beat her into submission, she never went down without a fight. She turned and placed her elbow in Tiffany's face.

Tiffany screamed as Jane grabbed her and slammed her against the wall with her arm twisted behind her back.

Danny charged in. “What’s going on?”

“That bitch broke my nose,” Tiffany said. “And this one’s trying to break my arm.”

Ethan cried, so Lacy picked him up to soothe him. Johnny rushed into the room followed by Nick, Liz, and Mrs. Baker.

Nick started crying when he saw his mom’s nose bleeding. Lacy felt like horse hockey. She hated violence…or rather, hated being the victim of it. When threatened, she reacted like she always had, determined to fight to the death. The difference was this time, since she’d had some training, she’d actually done the damage she’d intended to do. It had been too much.

Danny got a towel for Tiffany’s nose. Jane had released her, but was poised to take control of the situation if the need should arise. Johnny held Nick who was still crying.

“Can I take him?” Liz reached for Ethan.

Lacy passed her son to her and clenched her fists by her side to keep them from shaking.

“Jane, did you see what happened?” Mrs. Baker asked.

“Yes. Why don’t we get Nick something to drink?” Jane said.

“Mommy, are you okay?” Nick asked between whimpers.

She looked at Nick with contempt, making Lacy glad she’d connected the blow.

“Your mama will be fine, son,” Johnny said.

Lacy needed to get out of the room. "I'll take Nick for some… What do you think, Nick? Hot chocolate?"

He sniffed and nodded before Johnny set him down. He took Lacy's hand, but looked back as they left the room.

***

Johnny's face was hotter than the fire in the pit out back. He took a few deep breaths to calm himself and made sure Lacy, Nick, Liz, and Ethan were down the stairs before he turned his attention back to his ex-wife. She made him want to spit.

"What happened?" he asked.

Jane explained and Tiffany's eyes narrowed in defiance as a towel covered most of her face.

"I'm going to sue." She sounded like a telephone operator from the days of old.

"Tif, if you need your nose fixed, I'll pay for it, but I don't think a lawsuit is necessary," Johnny said.

"Yeah," Danny added. "You came here uninvited and attacked a woman. She defended herself. No judge is going to award you a settlement for getting your nose busted under those circumstances. In fact, it could damage your custodial privileges."

"What? No, she started it." She pointed at the open door. "She told my son I was selfish."

"No, she didn't," Johnny said. "She told him sometimes parents could be selfish."

"She was speaking about her own mother," Mama D said. "If Nick said anything different, then he misunderstood. Since when is it okay to attack a woman, no matter what you mistakenly thought she said? I think custody should be questioned—"

"Mama D." Johnny shook his head. "There's no need for that. Nick needs a relationship with his mother. At least until he's old enough to make his own decisions." He turned his gaze back to Tiffany. "Maybe by then, he'll feel loved by you enough to want to stay in touch."

"What do you mean?" Tiffany asked.

"I've talked to you about this before. If you can't see how much Nick wants your approval, then I can't help you. *I* gave up wanting your approval a long time ago, but Nick still needs you."

"But, Johnny, can't you forgive me? Can't we try to be family again?" She gripped the front of his shirt with both fists.

Her nose was no longer bleeding, and the pleading in her eyes touched a place deep inside him. A place he'd closed off a long time ago.

A fist of internal fury slammed into his stomach. Tiffany had used him and told him to his face no woman could ever love a fool like him.

For the second time that night, he pried her hands off his chest. "That ship has sailed, darlin'." He intended the term of endearment to be derogatory.

His brother, sister-in-law, and mom said nothing, but nodded their approval.

"Danny, could I trouble you to take Tiffany to the hospital if she wants to go? I need to check on Nick and let him know everything's okay."

Johnny went downstairs and scanned the throng of costumes. Neither Nick nor Lacy were in sight.

Jen touched his sleeve. “They went to your cottage, sweetie. Liz and Ethan, too.”

He found all four of them in Nick’s bed. They were crowded and cozy.

“Is he asleep?” Johnny unhooked his cape and laid it on a chair with his helmet and sword.

With Lacy’s arm draped over him, Nick rested on his side next to a sleeping Ethan.

Liz nodded. “These boys are worn out.”

Johnny touched Lacy’s shoulder. “Are you okay?”

She rolled onto her back. “Yeah. I’ve had my hair pulled before. It’s never fun, but it hasn’t killed me yet.” She started to sit up. “Here, I’ll move so you can be next to him.”

Johnny helped her stand.

“I’m not going anywhere until Tiffany’s gone,” Liz said. “Ethan has a clean diaper thanks to Lacy, so we might just crash here, little brother.”

“That’s fine. Y’all can have my bed if you want. I want to be with Nick.”

“He was upset at first,” Liz said, “but Lacy told him it was a misunderstanding, and she was sorry.”

“It wasn’t your fault, Lacy.” He slid his arms around her. “It shouldn’t have happened. I’m so sorry she attacked you.”

“If you’d seen me throw that elbow, you might’ve been proud.” She leaned back, her arms around his waist.

He chuckled, despite his dark mood. “Definitely, Little Bit.” He pulled her close again. “Give her a few minutes to clear out before you go back over there. I don't want any more confrontations tonight, although it'd be fun to see one of the world's smallest Stormtroopers kick stripper Leia's butt."

Lacy and Liz both laughed, and Nick stirred.

"Miss Lacy." He sat up and wrapped his arms around her waist from behind. "Will you stay here with me tonight?"

She released Johnny and turned to hug Nick. "I wish. But I have to go clean up the party, and you're gonna have an even better bedfellow than me. Your dad's gonna stay with you."

"He snores." Nick pouted.

"So do I," she said. "You'll never get any sleep with both of us snoring in your ears." She made an obnoxious noise, like pigs after slop. "You want me to save you some mummy dogs, if there are any leftover?"

"Yes, ma'am." He squeezed her tighter. "I love you, Miss Lacy."

Lacy pressed her lips to the top of Nick's head. "I love you, too. And don't you forget it."

Johnny's heart beat faster than it had when a ghost he'd forgotten about fell from a tree and landed on top of him. He swallowed down the emotion rising in his throat. It had to be love.

When Lacy backed up, without thinking of the consequences Johnny slid his arms around her again. She stiffened initially, then slowly relaxed into him, putting her hands on top of his for a moment.

Reluctantly, he released her. From the door, she offered a small smile and a wave before disappearing from view.

"I shouldn't have done that, Lizabelle," he said quietly to his sister.

"Don't be so sure, Johnny boy." She cocked an eyebrow.

Chapter Fifteen

By the time Lacy returned to the main house, the party had dwindled. Mrs. Baker and Jen were sending food home with some of the guests. Maddie was washing serving trays.

Mr. Baker sidled up next to Lacy and put his arm around her. "I'm going to give you a Halloween bonus. We'll call it hazard pay."

"Yeah," Maddie said. "I've been wanting to smash Tiffany's face for years. I'm just sorry you beat me to it."

"Mad, I'm surprised you haven't, as feisty as you are." Paul held his sleeping son in his arms.

"You've done a wonderful job with everything." Mrs. Baker put an arm around Lacy. "We'll clean up. You can sit with us. Or if you're as worn out as you should be, go on to your cottage and rest."

Assuming the family wanted some time together without an outsider, Lacy excused herself.

At her cabin, she discarded her costume and took a hot bath.

When she was drying off, there was a knock at her door. Thinking it might be Liz again, rather than struggle into clothes before she was dry, Lacy wrapped the towel around her and opened the door.

Johnny stood there, staring down at her near nakedness for the longest seconds of her life before he turned his back to her. "Sorry." He cleared his throat. "I went to the house, and they, ah, told me you were here."

She hesitated, unsure whether to invite him in or keep him waiting on the stoop.

"I thought you were Liz. I'm sorry I didn't dress first. Give me a minute, okay?" She left the door open, while she went to the bedroom.

"Take your time." He stayed outside.

The strong smell of his soap let her know he'd recently showered off his Darth Vader persona.

His touch had preoccupied her thoughts for the last half hour. She was sure it hadn't meant anything. It had been an emotional moment, and Nick had been upset. Lacy had been rattled from the confrontation and imagined Johnny would be affected a hundredfold.

Once dressed, she joined him on the porch. Johnny slid over on the bench, so Lacy could sit next to him. Their arms touched and he took her hand.

"I wanted to apologize for Tiffany. Are you sure you're okay?"

His hand was big and warm. The realization that she didn't want him to let go sent a chill up her arm. When she shivered, he let go of her hand and put his arm around her.

"I'm fine, Johnny. I'm more worried about Nick…and you." It felt so natural to lean into him, but she tried hard not to completely mold herself to his side.

"I'm ticked off, and Nick will be all right. I need to figure out how to help him handle it. Tiffany's always been a little unpredictable. I guess that was part of the appeal in the beginning. But I've always been a wild card too, so we just didn't work."

"You'll figure it out. It'd probably be best not to make a huge deal out of it, but I don't think Tiffany will allow that." The knot in Lacy's stomach, which had formed during the incident, hadn't gone away.

"I'll talk to her. I should've realized something was up. She broke up with her boyfriend last week and said some things about the way I look."

Lacy glanced up at him. "Good things?"

"Yeah. I didn't start taking care of myself for her, but she's the only female who's noticed."

"That's not true." Lacy clamped her mouth closed and looked away, heat flooding her face.

"Oh, yeah?" His voice rose on the last word, and he squeezed her arm a couple times.

"I just meant you haven't been around other women. At least, not that I know of."

"Is that all you meant?" He grinned. "This is your fault, you know? If you hadn't been starving me for the last six weeks, I'd still be my old fat happy self."

"You weren't fat, and *you're* the one who started exercising. I didn't make you do that."

"But you may have inspired me." The warmth of his body radiated into hers.

"How?" She held a hand up. "Wait—don't answer that. I may be misreading this situation. I'm really bad at male/female stuff, so I think I should tell you this feels…flirty. I work for your family. I'm not interested in looking for a new job because I didn't speak up when I should have."

He took his arm from around her, and a chill replaced his heat.

"I didn't mean to make you uncomfortable. I wasn't flirting. Just being…friendly. I mean, you may work here, but we're friends, aren't we?"

She leaned her shoulder into his arm and nudged him. "Yes, we're friends. I don't have many of those, so thank you."

"Thank you for being honest with me…and for loving my son." His voice cracked.

Lacy blinked and turned away, pretending to hear a sound in the woods. She wasn't being honest with Johnny or herself. Nick wasn't the only one she loved, but she couldn't risk everything by revealing the truth. A partial truth would have to suffice.

"Johnny, I love all your family, and I'll do whatever I can for any of you. You know that, right?"

"I know, Little Bit. You're the best thing that could've happened to Southland. We're lucky to have you."

She smiled and leaned her head against his

arm, knowing she was sending mixed signals, but desiring closeness and comfort. The nickname he called her from time to time was starting to grow on her, even though she'd always hated being reminded of her short stature. Johnny made her feel valued and protected, rather than small and insignificant. All the Bakers made her feel important. It wasn't something she was used to, but she liked it.

"I better get to bed, so I can feed the army tomorrow morning. Give Nick a kiss for me."

"You have to give me a kiss to give him."

"Huh?" Her heart drummed a new rhythm as a battle waged between her body and her brain.

***

Johnny whistled all the way back to his cottage. The warm imprint of her sweet lips still lingered on his cheek. When he'd noticed Lacy's distress, he'd pointed to his cheek and said, "Put your lips right here."

In his living room, he found Liz reading, or rather staring at photographs in his *Men's Fitness* magazine. He'd tossed it in the trash because of who was on the cover. Ian Clarke was the movie star who'd broken her heart and given her the love of her life.

Johnny glanced through the open bedroom door to see Nick and Ethan still sleeping soundly. He sat next to his sister and put his arm around her. "That boy of yours is precious, Lizabelle."

"He is, isn't he? He has my whole heart, Johnny. I never imagined I could love anyone so much."

He knew exactly what she meant. "We miss you now that you live so far away."

"It's not that far, and you know you're welcome to come see us anytime. In fact, you better bring Nick when school's out." Liz lightly pounded her fist just above his knee.

"If I leave for any length of time, I have to get someone out here to do the chores." He propped his feet on the coffee table.

"Lacy'll do 'em. Especially, if Mama D and Big Daddy come with you. She won't have as much to do in the house, so she can feed the horses and muck the stalls." Her face held no expression as she watched him.

Clenching his teeth, he bit back his retort. Why did it make him mad to picture Lacy doing the hard manual labor? When Liz cut her eyes and turned up one side of her mouth, the tension drained from his shoulders. She'd been testing him, wanting him to show his true feelings.

"Always the sly one, aren't you, sister?"

"It's no secret to any of us, Johnny. The way you look at her says it all."

"Then I'll have to be more careful. She made it clear she's our employee, and I'm to stop flirting with her."

"Put you in your place, did she?"

"From the first day we met." He smiled. "And every day since."

Liz laughed with him. "You've met your match then."

***

The next morning, chaos at breakfast meant

business as usual at Southland. The kids were chasing each other around the table as the adults fixed plates and tried to herd them into chairs.

Lacy stood at the sink, bouncing one of the twins on her hip. Dillon, the baby girl, giggled, and Johnny moved closer to hear Lacy humming a nursery rhyme.

"Mornin', Miss Lacy," he said, fighting a smile.

"Hey. How's Nick?"

"He's fine. We had a little talk. Sometimes, grownups have bad days and do dumb stuff."

Lacy smiled and nodded at him. "Good man."

Running into the kitchen, Nick headed straight for Lacy and wrapped his arms around her waist. Johnny took the baby from her to free her hands, and she hugged Nick back.

"Lacy," Liz said. "When Johnny and Nick come to visit us at the beach, you have to come with them. Bring your suit because we're right on the water, and the kids are ankle deep in sand all day long."

Johnny left them talking, while he supervised Nick getting food and tossed his niece into the air. "Danny, you and Jane make pretty babies. You going to have more?"

"I don't know, bro. Two are a handful. I'm grateful Lizabelle is there to help out when I'm in L.A. Maybe when Dillon and Davis are a little older, you know, potty trained." Danny held out his hands and Johnny passed the baby. "What about you? Gonna get back together with Tiffany and make your family proud?"

About to supply one of his smartass answers, Johnny jumped when a sippy cup of milk exploded all over his feet.

Lacy stood with open hands and an open mouth. "I'm so sorry." She turned to grab kitchen towels.

Johnny took one of the two towels she held, and they both bent to clean the mess. They butted heads, and Lacy fell backward on her keister, landing in the milk. Her hand cupped her head.

Johnny knelt and put his hand on top of hers. "I'm so sorry, sweetheart. Are you okay?"

"I know you aren't supposed to cry over spilled milk," she said, "but ouch."

He gripped her elbow. "Let me help you up."

She waved him away. "I might as well mop up while I'm down here."

"Lacy, I'd go ahead and take some Advil if I were you." Danny chuckled. "Johnny's hardheaded, so you'll be having a headache soon."

"You must know from experience," she said.

"Yep." Danny stepped around them toward the table.

Johnny stayed down to help her clean the mess. He handed the cup and lid to Jane and crawled on his hands and knees to wipe the spots, which had splattered the farthest. While he was on all fours, Nick climbed on his back. It set off a chain reaction where Tyler and Ethan also tried to climb on.

"Kids, we have actual horses you can ride," Liz said. "Get off of him."

Lacy giggled. "I need new pants."

"What? You don't like having a soggy

bottom?" Johnny asked.

Laughing, the boys ran off on another wild child chase through the house. Johnny stood and lifted Lacy off the floor. He had to stop himself from patting her wet butt as she walked away.

Chapter Sixteen

As Lacy walked to her cottage for a change of clothes, she thought about what Danny had said. She'd been under the impression the family disliked Tiffany, but she could see how it would be good for Nick to have his parents together.

A wave of disappointment nearly knocked her over. Had Johnny been trying to tell her the night before when she'd interrupted him? She'd completely misinterpreted his friendly gestures as flirting. When it came to men, she'd probably always be clueless.

She wondered if Johnny and Nick would move to Atlanta or if Tiffany would move to Southland. If she did, Lacy would have to polish her résumé and find another job. Maybe she could be a nanny if the Bakers gave her a good reference. Liz made coastal Georgia sound amazing.

After she showered off the sticky milk and put on fresh clothes, she walked back toward the main house. Most of the Bakers were at the barn, saddling horses for another ride.

"You wanna try?" Johnny asked as she passed.

"I've been a klutz already today. I'm afraid the horses won't be safe around me." She smiled as she tentatively touched the neck of the horse called Bo.

With everyone there, Lacy was even less inclined to try riding. If she fell off or peed her pants, there would be too many witnesses to her shame. She'd also run out of pants.

"Come on, Miss Lacy," Nick said. "Bo likes her, Dad. She can ride him, and I'll ride Luke."

"Do you mean like the Duke boys?" she asked.

"Yes, ma'am. We also have Uncle Jessie and Daisy."

Lacy laughed. "I'm not sure having Bo Duke try to eat my hair is enough to convince me he likes me. He's so big."

"You should give it a try," Liz said. "Johnny will help, and he won't let anything happen to you. I'm taking Ethan with me on Daisy Duke. Yeehaw." She wriggled her eyebrows as her son stomped around in the dirt, wearing tiny cowboy boots.

Looking at Lacy with raised eyebrows, Johnny gave her a crooked grin. She got the feeling that agreeing to ride would make his day. He'd had a rough time the night before.

She took a deep breath. Maybe it was time for a new adventure. "Okay."

"Yeehaw," Johnny said, and Nick and a few others joined in the cheer.

"You guys ride ahead," Johnny told them. "I'm gonna lead her around the corral a bit. Make sure she's comfortable."

Lacy turned her attention to the horse. "It's a good thing you're Bo Duke. I had a crush on him when I was little. I was going to be Mrs. Bo Duke when I grew up." She dropped her voice to a whisper. "The difference is if for some reason I wind up on the ground, I don't want you on top of me. Got it?"

It might've been her imagination, but she swore the horse laughed at her. It certainly had a twinkle in its eye.

***

Johnny took a few deep breaths to settle down. It wasn't often he got tickled pink, as Aunt May used to say. Lacy agreeing to ride surprised him. Liz would be getting a Johnny bear hug for plugging him as the one to help Lacy.

It only took a few minutes to explain the tack and what each thing was for. He showed her how to mount. When she did, her eyes were as big as saucers, and she had a death grip on the pommel.

"You're fine. Take a breath and relax. I don't even think Bo knows he has a rider. What are you, a buck?"

"A buck?" Her forehead wrinkled.

"Your weight?"

"Now, you know your mama would spank you if she knew you asked me that. I don't go around asking your weight."

His grin got bigger. "You're right. I wasn't thinking, and honestly, I didn't think you'd be offended. I mean if I weighed a hundred pounds…" He shook his head. "Never mind, bad example.

Please accept my sincere apologies." He performed an exaggerated bow.

She chuckled. "Change of subject. How do I steer this mammoth?"

He led her around until she was ready to take the reins. She got Bo going, and Johnny mounted Uncle Jessie, glad he was already tacked up. He guided his horse next to her.

"I didn't think of it before, but you could've just ridden with me," he said.

Her head tilted to the side. "That doesn't sound very fun."

It would be for me. He needed to get over his crush on Lacy. She'd made it clear the previous night she wouldn't put up with any funny business.

"You ready to take this party out on a trail?"

She nodded, and he led his horse through the gate. They rode on the lane, which was wide enough to ride side by side.

Just when Lacy began to look comfortable, the thundering sound of a horse running shook the earth. The faint screams of a woman heightened Johnny's senses.

A moment later, twelve-year-old Beth galloped past on Pookie, one of the Appaloosas who spooked rather easily. Beth wasn't as comfortable on horseback as the other kids, because she lived in Atlanta and rarely rode anymore due to her beauty pageant queen duties. Just like her mama, Katie.

Maddie was giving chase from her mount, but she had no lariat. Johnny's hung from the saddle, so he nudged Jessie into high gear. He started through the woods in the direction Pookie was already running and gradually maneuvered his horse to close the distance.

"She won't stop, Uncle Johnny," Beth yelled.

Considering his options, he yelled to Maddie, "The creek."

It was open there, and they could herd Pookie and get her to slow down. And Johnny could possibly, if he was lucky, get the catch rope to land where he willed it. Grabbing the horse's front foot was not an option because Beth would fly like Superman over the horse's head.

"Bethie, when I start slowing her down, hold on. She may rear up."

In one smooth toss, he got the rope around Pookie's neck and got out in front a little. He started slowing Jessie down, and to his relief, Pookie slowed her pace until they came to a full stop.

Too close for Beth to dismount, Johnny pulled her off of her horse and onto his lap.

They switched horses, and Johnny rode Pookie back to where he'd last seen Lacy. When he remembered he'd left her, his stomach tied itself in a knot. Acting without thinking again.

He found her with everyone else at the barn. They'd decided to cut their ride short. Jane told him Danny had caught Lacy when she nearly fell off of Bo while dismounting. Johnny pursed his lips as envy grabbed hold of him. If he could be a hero like his brother, maybe a woman would fall in love with him.

After getting off his horse, he forced the air out of his lungs, and checked on Lacy.

"You're to be hailed as the savior of the hour."

Lacy curtsied. "I'll make your favorite treat as a reward."

The only reward he wanted was a kiss. Maybe on the lips this time. But he'd have to settle for a German Chocolate upside-down cake.

***

Lacy practically went weak in the knees. Johnny was like a real cowboy, and the warm feelings she had toward him before were only amplified by seeing him rescue his niece from a runaway horse. She didn't actually *see* the whole thing, but when he'd left her side, he was a man on a rescue mission.

After making his favorite dessert, she was glad the family was there to help them eat it. They needed to get the Halloween candy out of the house and get back to healthy meals and snacks. She really was the food police as Johnny and Mr. Baker jokingly called her.

"That was delicious." Johnny rinsed his dirty plate in the sink.

"Let me." She tried to take it from him. "We should think of non-food rewards in the future."

"I can think of one." He waggled his eyebrows.

She narrowed her eyes at him, trying to be tough. "I'm open to all suggestions, but tread carefully."

He puckered his lips, and heat raced up her neck. If he asked for a kiss, she might abandon her principles and give in.

"Sing for me."

"Ha." Relief belayed her disappointment. "That wouldn't be a reward. It'd be torture. I can't sing."

"You lie." He exaggerated the L-sound, making the word breathy and exceptionally ominous.

Her lips twisted. "Dangit."

"You're a terrible liar."

She lifted her chin. "I'll take that as a compliment."

"As you should. Next time I do something really brave, I get a song. Deal?"

She studied his extended hand for a minute, trying to decide if she was willing to give such a private part of herself to him. She'd given into Nick on the subject, but was she also willing to trust Johnny with her voice?

Most people would think the debate raging in her mind was insignificant, but Stan had told her so many times not to quit her day job she figured he must've been right. According to him, she couldn't sing to save her life.

"Any other ideas?" she asked.

His hand dropped to his side. "None that won't get me in trouble, but I'll think on it."

She hated to disappoint him, but she'd almost rather risk a kiss than sing for him.

Chapter Seventeen

On Monday, Lacy was dicing potatoes for chowder when Heath came in the back door wearing his uniform. He was a big dude, and the uniform brought back bad memories. She shuddered and looked away.

Jane had just put the twins in their bouncy swings, and Heath went over to tickle their chins. They'd be returning home the next day, and Lacy would miss their sweet little baby noises. The smelly diapers, not so much.

"Lacy, I have some bad news." Heath stood and walked over to the counter. "My dad just called me, and Tiffany is pressing charges. A judge just issued a warrant for your arrest."

The knife she held slipped, and she caught it as it fell, slicing her palm.

"Dixie," Jane called. "Is the first aid kit still under the sink?"

Lacy ran the cut under cold water. It wasn't

deep, but it was long.

Mrs. Baker came into the kitchen and doctored Lacy's hand.

"Heath, I want to go in. I don't want them to come here."

"I told my dad I'd bring you in. You may have to stay in lockup for a few hours, but since it's Monday, we should have you home in time for supper."

"I'll call my sister, Nancy. She's an attorney." Mrs. Baker placed strips of surgical tape on the side of the counter.

"This is bullshit." Jane crossed her arms over her chest. "Pardon my language."

"Johnny went to Atlanta to try to talk Tiffany out of the very thing she's already done," Mrs. Baker said.

"I don't think we should tell him until after we bond her out," Heath said. "He'll lose it."

"You're right," Mrs. Baker said.

"What about Nick? If I'm not here when he gets home…" Lacy said.

Mrs. Baker placed gauze over the cut and taped it down. "I'll tell him you cut your hand and went to the doctor."

"I'll go with them if you can watch the kids, Mama D," Jane said. "I'm going to make a statement for the record. And Lacy, I think you should file for a restraining order against Tiffany since she attacked you. Nancy can help with that."

Lacy shook her head. "That won't stop her if she wants to come after me."

"You're right, but if you show you can take

legal action too, she may change her mind and drop the charges."

As they drove to the sheriff's office, Jane looked over at her. "You speak about restraining orders like someone who's been there. Is there anything we should know?"

Lacy thought about it. Nothing in her past had anything to do with the current situation, but she had a bad feeling it was going to come out whether she wanted it to or not.

She sighed. "I tried it once. Took out a restraining order on someone."

"And?"

"It only made things worse." *And endangered the people I love.* That was all she intended to say about the subject.

Heath and Jane exchanged glances. Heath cleared his throat. "Have you ever been arrested?"

"No."

"Well, you're lucky this is a small town," Heath said. "They'll keep you in lockup at the local office. It shouldn't be crowded, and my dad will make sure you're as comfortable as possible."

"One of us will be here to get you as soon as we can get you bonded out," Jane said.

"Thank you both for being so nice." Lacy leaned back against the seat and closed her eyes, holding her breath to keep down the fear that had settled like a rock in the pit of her stomach.

***

Johnny knocked on the door to the house he and Tiffany had once shared. He'd given it to her as part of the divorce settlement. That and a hefty alimony check. But since they'd signed a pre-nup, he knew what he'd been getting into. He'd been naive enough to think he'd never need the protection it gave him. They legally had shared custody of Nick, and he didn't mind paying child support. He was happy to provide for his son and glad he had the means.

Tiffany worked odd jobs like waitressing and bartending, but did it for the social outlet it provided. She didn't really need the money. Not as long as Johnny kept forking it over.

His current salary wasn't anywhere near what it had been when he was second-in-command of his father's company. He still had his trust fund, his investments, and his trees, but he liked living beneath his means. It was important for Nick to learn to work hard for what he got and not expect handouts. Nick wouldn't have access to his trust fund until he turned thirty, just like the rest of the Baker kids.

Tiffany opened the door. "Johnny, this is a nice surprise." She had a piece of tape over her nose.

"I wanted to check on you. Make sure you're all right."

"Come in. It's not broken, but it hurts like hell. I'm using a special painkiller. Works like magic. Want some?" She held up a bottle of tequila.

If he was gonna carry out his plan of seduction, he was gonna need a drink. "I'll get the salt and lime."

They clanked shot glasses and threw the first one back.

After he sucked the lime, he said, "We're

gonna fire Lacy. She'll have to go back to North Carolina where she came from. I'd like to make sure she doesn't have any charges against her that would hinder her leaving."

"Good riddance. What are you going to do for me, Johnny?" She moved into his personal space and gave the lime a slow lick.

He stroked Tiffany's long, dark hair as he spoke. "What do you want?"

"You."

"Do you need to call anybody before we get this party started?"

"Give me a minute." She picked up her phone and stepped out of the room. She came back a few minutes later. "Taken care of."

He poured them both another shot.

They started in the kitchen, and after two more shots, Tiffany was on him like stink on shit. They moved to the bedroom where Johnny had to take a break.

He nearly came unglued. "You have a stripper pole? Has Nick seen this?"

"Yes, he thinks it's exercise equipment, which it is." She leaned against the pole and arched her back. "Do you want a show?"

Johnny had to look away and choke down his anger. "Wow me."

"Take off your shirt and sit back on the bed."

While he unbuttoned his shirt slowly, her gaze followed his fingers, and she licked her lips. When he let it drop to the floor, she stepped close to him and rubbed her hands down his chest.

"You look better now than you ever did,

Johnny. I always knew you had abs under that flab."

He raised his eyebrows. The backhanded compliments weren't doing anything for his libido, which was non-existent at the moment.

She went into the bathroom, and he settled himself on the bed, sitting up and leaning against the padded headboard. He looked at his crotch. "You better respond when you're needed."

Tiffany came out wearing sheer lingerie and high heels. The tape was missing from her nose. She turned on some music and began a stripper routine.

Johnny fought a yawn and tried to look interested. He'd rather file his nails with sandpaper, but he kept his gaze locked on her. She did have a nice body since she worked out with a personal trainer. And the boobs he bought her after Nick was born still looked good. He'd never gotten used to the way they felt though, and the memory of it almost made him curl his lip.

Focus, Baker. What did turned on look like? Hooded eyes? Open mouth? Drool? He reached for the tequila and drank from the bottle. This was harder than he thought.

With all of the touching and teasing she was doing, Tiffany was turning herself on. Johnny had to think about how to get turned on, too. Unbidden, Lacy's face popped into his head, and he was powerless to push it out.

Tiffany crawled onto the bed wearing nothing but a thong and those damned high heels. She rubbed herself on him, starting at his feet and working her way up. This would work if she were

Lacy.

He forced her out of his mind. He couldn't screw his ex-wife while thinking about another woman. Tiffany moved to kiss his lips, and he stopped her.

"My turn." He got up from the bed and moved to the stripper pole.

She took his place on the bed, sipped tequila from the bottle, and watched with a wry smile as he performed his own striptease. It was easy to get out of his jeans since they were loose on him. He kicked the jeans to the side and shook his butt at her. Since he wore camouflaged boxer shorts, he pretended he was invisible.

Just when he started to climb on the bed, the doorbell rang. *Thank God.*

His joystick was not cooperating, and Tiffany was seconds away from discovering that little tidbit of information.

Sliding out of bed, she put on a robe. Johnny put his jeans and shirt back on. He peeked around the corner, while waiting to see who he needed to thank for the interruption.

"Todd, what are you doing here?" Tiffany tightened the belt of her robe.

"Do you have company?"

"Johnny's here," she said.

Johnny stepped into his boots, not wanting Tif's most recent ex-boyfriend to find him in any state of undress.

"What does that tub of lard want?" Todd stepped into the house.

Tiffany fidgeted. "We were talking about Nick.

What are you doing here?"

"I missed you, baby." Todd pulled Tiffany tight against his body and cupped her butt.

Johnny cleared his throat as he walked into view. Todd shifted Tiffany to his side and kept a hand on her hip. Tiffany's arm went around his waist.

"Johnny, good to see you." Todd extended his hand.

"Uh-huh. Good talk, Tiffany." He cupped himself and walked past them, out the door.

***

They really rolled out the welcome at the sheriff's department. Lacy was greeted by Heath's father and then booked for assault.

How ironic.

They left her in the women's holding area with the door open, and they offered her drinks and snacks. It was almost like visiting distant relatives.

Lacy's fear had died down a little, until Sheriff Cook had to step out of the office. He closed her in the cell, and she was all alone with her thoughts and a newspaper.

The deputy on duty gave her the creeps. He paced in front of the door, leering at her when he thought she wasn't looking.

"You know," he stopped outside the door, hands on his hips, "sometimes, we leave the door open for our special friends."

Lacy looked at him but didn't respond. He was implying something, and she didn't want to think too hard about what it was. Maybe Heath's dad closed her in for her safety.

"You'd have to make it very special though." He adjusted his crotch.

Subtle. To anyone watching, it would look like he was doing that thing men always do.

"No thanks." She turned back to examine the well-worn newspaper, which she'd already read front to back and back to front.

The lock tumbled, and she closed her eyes. He was going to push the issue. Another man with power over someone abusing that power. Typical of the law enforcement types she'd encountered in the past.

"Don't you want to be my friend?" he asked. "I'll treat you right, little lady." His narrow shoulders blocked most of the doorway. "You have a sweet mouth. I bet you know how to make a man happy with that mouth." Judging by the bulge in his pants, he was talking himself up.

She tossed the paper down as her ire rose to its full height. "I'm not doing you any *special* favors, Deputy. If you want something from me, you're going to have to take it by force like the criminal you are."

"Now, wait just a damn minute. Do you know who you're talking to?" He took a step toward her.

"Do you know who *you're* talking to?" a voice asked from behind him.

Chapter Eighteen

As soon as Johnny walked in the door at Southland, Danny passed one of the twins to him. He didn't see Lacy right away and got distracted when Nick came in with Liz.

"How was school, buddy?"

"Good. Where's Miss Lacy?" Nick asked.

Johnny looked to Mama D and noticed the glances she and Danny exchanged. Johnny cocked his head.

"Lacy cut her hand, and Jane took her to the doctor," Mama D said. "She'll be back in a little while."

Liz picked Ethan up. "Nick, let's go play in the playroom."

Heath came in the back door. "Johnny, you're back."

Johnny shifted the baby in his arms. "What's going on?"

"Let me take him." Mama D held out her

hands.

Johnny passed the baby and then clenched his fists. While they told him about Lacy, he paced the floor. “Why didn’t somebody call me?”

“There was nothing you could do, Johnny.” Heath tried to reason with him.

“Like hell. I got Tiffany to call her lawyer. I think she’s dropped the charges, but I can’t be sure since you guys left me out of the loop.”

“Look, my dad’s with her,” Heath said. “I’ll call him, and he’ll give you an update. She’s fine. You’ll see.”

Johnny listened as Heath called his father.

“Who’s on duty?” There was silence. “Dad, Cox is creepy. I’m going down there.”

Heath clipped his phone onto his belt. “Shit fire and save matches. Come on, Johnny.” He bolted for the door.

Johnny didn’t have to ask about the creep. Deputy Cox had a reputation for frisking the females a little too thoroughly when he made arrests. The problem was most of them were drunk, so their complaints weren’t taken seriously.

They met the sheriff at the back door to the office, and he led them down the hall toward the open door of the cell. The sheriff stopped, held out his arm, and turned, placing his finger over his lips.

They stood stark still and listened. Johnny nearly lost it when Cox talked about Lacy’s sweet mouth. Heath put a hand on his chest to restrain him.

When the sheriff finally interrupted the deputy’s tirade, it took all of Heath’s muscle mass to keep Johnny from ripping the man apart.

"Dad's finally got him, Shake and Bake. This means he can ax the pervert."

"Give me your gun and badge, Cox. You're fired."

"But, Sheriff, you should've seen this little slut teasing me with those pouty lips. It wasn't my fault."

"Miss Lacy, would you like to press harassment charges against former Deputy Cox? I can probably get a dozen sworn statements in addition to yours."

After the sheriff and Heath took Cox out of the cell, Johnny could finally get in to see Lacy.

He sat next to her, pulled her onto his lap, and hugged her close. "I'm so sorry about all of this."

She sniffed and wiped her eyes.

"Just wipe it on my shirt. I'm so used to tears and snot, it doesn't faze me anymore. In fact, I think Davis spit up on me just before I left Southland."

She shook with laughter. "You smell good, like soap."

"You smell like prison," he said. "It's like a mix of Cheetos and beer farts."

Her laughter turned to tears.

"Oh, sweetheart. That's not how you smell, just this room."

"I ate Cheetos for lunch." She sobbed.

"Shh." He rocked and patted her. "Lacy, baby, you're gonna be all right. I won't let anything happen to you. I'm trying to fix this thing with Tiffany."

Even if it meant he had to sleep with the

enemy. If Tiffany got what she really wanted, if she thought she'd won, she'd relent.

"Guess who's here?" Heath said from the door. "Nancy just walked in, but so did Tiffany and her lawyer. Let's cross our fingers that she'll sign a waiver of prosecution. You should be going home very soon, Lacy."

"Tiffany doesn't need to know I'm here," Johnny said. "I promised her something if she would let this go, and my being here won't look good for our cause."

"We'll go out the back," Heath said.

"I'll see you at Southland." Johnny hugged Lacy close and kissed the top of her head. He didn't want to leave her there, but if Tiffany knew, she'd never drop the charges.

***

"Lacy, I'm sorry we haven't met before now. I'm Nancy. I've heard great things about you." She handed Lacy a piece of paper. "This is a temporary restraining order against Tiffany Baker. There'll be a hearing at which time the judge will decide to extend it or not."

Lacy stared at the document, but couldn't make sense of the jumble of letters.

"I'd like to drive you back to Southland, so we can talk," Nancy said. "Jane's still here, so she'll ride with us."

"She waited here all this time?" Lacy's spirits lifted a little.

"Yes, of course. She was worried about you. Everyone was."

Lacy slid into the passenger seat of Nancy's

Mercedes, and Jane sat in the back. It was Lacy's first time in a luxury car. The leather seats were soft, and it smelled expensive.

"I don't know how much it costs to have a lawyer." Lacy fidgeted.

"Honey, I'd pay you to let me represent you against Tiffany. Don't even worry about it. Plus, I think Johnny's going to pay her off or something."

"Does Johnny have a lot of money?"

Jane laughed, and Nancy looked at her with a smirk. "In case you hadn't noticed, the Bakers are pretty well off."

"They just seem so…normal." Lacy's voice sounded small to her own ears.

"That's what I thought, too," Jane said.

"They are extremely unpretentious," Nancy said. "But you must know normal people can't afford houses, horses, land, planes, and multiple vehicles."

Lacy nodded. Since she'd been with the Bakers for more than six weeks, the novelty of their toys had worn off, and she just saw them for who they were, the salt of the earth.

"Lacy, tell me about Stanley Riggs," Nancy said.

Blinking quickly, Lacy took a deep breath. *Busted.* "What about him?"

"The nature of your relationship."

As hard as Lacy tried not to be affected, a vice gripped her chest. "We don't have a relationship anymore. He's in prison for attempted murder. Mine. There were also some drug related charges, but I think those were dropped in the plea deal."

"How old were you when you met him?" Nancy's eyes were on the road.

"Sixteen."

"Where was your mother?" She cut her eyes.

Lacy's throat grew thick. "Drunk."

"So, you pretty much raised yourself then? I'd say you turned out really well, considering."

"You barely know me." Lacy rubbed the smooth leather of the seat on either side of her legs.

"I know enough. I can see how much Johnny cares for you."

"You're mistaken. Johnny and I are just friends. He's one of my employers, and anything more would be inappropriate."

Jane laughed again. "I sold myself that line for a long time, too."

Nancy didn't respond as she turned the car into Southland. Lacy leaned back against the seat and thought about Johnny. It had felt really good to be in his arms. Safe. She never would've let anyone else so close. With every passing day, he became more important to her, but there was no way he was in love with her. She had nothing to offer him.

When she got out of the car, Johnny was by her side in an instant. He picked her up in a bear hug.

"Johnny, put me down," she said as heat rose in her cheeks.

He did as she asked and pulled back to look at her. "What's wrong?"

"Johnny, Lacy, we need to go inside and talk," Nancy said.

When Lacy walked in, Nick greeted her with a big hug. "Mama D told me you got hurt. I'm glad you're home. Do you wanna play with me and Ethan?"

"Have you been eating sugar? You sure are hyper." She smoothed his hair.

He started nodding his head and jumping up and down.

"It's my fault," Liz said. "We drank Yoo-Hoos, and he's been bouncing off the walls ever since."

Lacy tweaked his nose. "We better find a way to expend some of that energy, so you can do your homework. You have school tomorrow, kiddo."

"Let's play the dance game." Jane herded the two boys into the other room.

"Yaaaaay!" Nick sang and began to dance around. Ethan copied his cousin.

Lacy rubbed her eyes. It had been a long day, and it was about to get longer.

"Let's sit." Nancy gestured to the table. Once Lacy, Johnny, Danny, Liz, and Mr. and Mrs. Baker were seated, she continued. "Tiffany's attorney says she will pursue a civil suit if Lacy stays."

Oh, no. I'm history. Tears she couldn't control fell, and she covered her face with her hands.

"Oh, honey." Mrs. Baker rubbed her back. "It's not so bad. We'll come up with a plan. It doesn't have to be forever. Does it, Nancy?"

"A few weeks should do the trick. Tiffany will calm down, and if she does pursue anything, we'll try to handle it with mediation."

"So, are we going to give Lacy a paid vacation?" Johnny asked.

"Why don't we have Thanksgiving in Florida this year?" Liz suggested. "My house will be ready in a couple weeks, and Lacy can fly back with us tomorrow. She can help with the kids and shopping and cooking."

"That's a great idea, Lizabelle," Mr. Baker said. "What do ya say, Lacy? A working vacation at the beach? I'll keep you on my payroll."

"Only, you have to at least pretend to work, just a little." Johnny held a small space between his finger and thumb.

"We'll be glad to have you, Lacy," Danny said. "And it's only for a little while. You'll be back up here by Christmas."

"Before," Mrs. Baker said. "I'm going to need help decorating."

"You should go pack," Liz said. "Don't forget swimwear and your Halloween costume. We're taking Ethan trick-or-treating Friday night."

The decision was made without Lacy ever saying a word. She should be thrilled, but the thought of leaving Southland…and Johnny and Nick made her heart hurt.

"What about Nick?" she asked Johnny. "Will he tell his mom I've only gone to Florida?"

"I'll tell him to say you're gone and only if she asks."

Chapter Nineteen

When Johnny explained about Lacy leaving for a few weeks, Nick got very upset. It wasn't surprising how attached his son had gotten to her in such a short time. With her loving nature and the nurturing she gave him, Nick was getting the things he missed from his real mother.

A tearful Nick raced to Lacy's cottage and when Johnny got there, she was rocking him on her lap. Nick sobbed as Lacy tried to comfort him. She re-explained everything and reminded him Thanksgiving was only four weeks away.

"Will you spend the night with me, Miss Lacy? I don't care if you snore."

She laughed. "If your dad says it's okay, but only this one time because I'm gonna miss you so much."

"Can she, Dad? She can sleep in my room." Nick wiped his face with the back of his arm.

Johnny rubbed his upper abdomen with the

palm of his hand to squelch the burning sensation. He hated seeing his son so upset, and he hated displacing Lacy.

"You're sure?" Johnny asked her, and she nodded.

Around midnight, Johnny woke up and went to check on Nick and Lacy. He smiled at the two of them sleeping, not a snore in earshot.

In the bathroom, he found Lacy's clothes folded neatly on the counter. He picked up her T-shirt and smelled the soothing lavender scent of the lotion she wore. Underneath, her white satiny bra enticed him.

Before he knew it, there was a pup tent in his pajama bottoms. He'd watched his ex-wife strip, and nothing had happened. One look at Lacy's bra, and his little soldier stood at attention. He was lost to a woman he could never have.

"Johnny."

He dropped her shirt like it had bitten him, and with his face on fire, he turned to her. She stood in the doorway wearing a cotton pajama set. The top was open, exposing a camisole.

When she saw him looking, she closed the front buttons of her shirt.

"I'm sorry I woke you," he said. "Thanks for spoiling my boy."

"He's a sweetheart. I don't know how you ever tell him no." She glanced toward the commode. "You didn't wake me. I've got to pee."

"Oh, sorry." He tried to exit while she was still blocking the doorway.

Her chest brushed his, and the tent was fully

pitched.

He paused. “Lacy.”

She stopped in front of him and looked up. He brushed the back of his finger lightly down her cheek, and she trembled. Slowly, he bent to kiss her.

“Dad? Miss Lacy? I woke up, and you were gone.” Nick held his blanket and rubbed his eyes.

“Just going to the bathroom.” She stepped inside the door and closed it.

“Bud, you better drain the lizard while you’re up.”

After Nick was finished in the bathroom, Johnny tucked him back into the bed next to Lacy.

When Johnny was at the door, Nick said, “Miss Lacy, hold my hand, please.”

“Did you wash it after you used the bathroom?” she asked.

Nick snorted. “Yes, ma’am.”

Lacy took his hand, and Johnny went back to bed with a smile on his face, despite his unfulfilled longing.

***

The next morning, Lacy contained her laughter as Nick pouted through breakfast. He overplayed his displeasure by shoving his lower lip out as far as it could go and exaggerating sighs meant to garner sympathy.

“Hey, Nick,” she said. “Can I drive you to the bus?”

He perked up a little.

Once they were in the golf cart on the way down the drive, she spoke. “I’m gonna miss you. I love you, Nick, and don't forget that, okay? You better make your dad call me, so we can talk sometimes."

"Okay, Miss Lacy. I know it's only temporary. I love you and I won't forget." He hugged her one last time and kissed her cheek before he got on the bus.

Later, they arrived at the airport and went to the hangar where the Bakers had not one, but two jets. Lacy didn't know the difference between a jet and any other kind of plane. It was a whole new world. She'd never flown before, and her stomach twisted into a French braid.

Danny was flying to Los Angeles for work, while Jane, Liz, and Lacy would be flying to the Georgia coast with the kids. It was a four-hour drive or just under an hour on a plane.

Lacy got hugs from Mr. and Mrs. Baker before she boarded the small plane. Johnny got on, carrying the luggage. Lacy chose an oversized leather seat next to a small window and sat down.

"You better get up from there and give me a hug, Little Bit." Johnny hovered over her in the compact space.

She started to push herself out of the seat, but he picked her up under her arms and set her on her feet.

"Don't forget me," he said, his body close but not quite touching hers.

Awareness of him lit a fire low in her belly. She let out a ragged breath and tried to step back, forgetting the seat behind her. He caught her before she fell, and then he kissed her…on the mouth…with just a little tongue.

This might have been the kiss they shared the night before if Nick hadn't interrupted when he had. She hadn't been able to go back to sleep for imagining it.

She melted into him until her rational brain resumed functioning. She broke the kiss by placing her palms on his chest and pushing gently. If she thought her breath was ragged before, she was wrong.

"W-what? Why did you do that?" She could hardly get the words out.

"So you won't forget me." He grinned and raised his brows once.

Her heart sped up even more. "I won't forget you, Johnny. B-but you shouldn't have…kissed me." *What was she saying?* It was the best kiss of her life, and she didn't want it to be the last.

"You guys want to finish your goodbye, so we can get this bird in the sky?" Jane asked.

Johnny started to back away, but Lacy stepped with him and wrapped her arms around him, pressing the side of her face into his chest. After a second, his arms went around her, too, and one of his hands stroked her hair and back. His lips brushed the top of her head, and she took it as her cue to let him go.

***

The only regret Johnny had about kissing Lacy was her not being around so he could do it again. She'd tasted so damn good he couldn't wait for more. He decided he didn't have to.

Friday morning, he confirmed his flight time

with his dad's pilot before working on last minute chores. He planned to drop Nick off with his mom for the weekend and then head to the coast and surprise Lacy.

Around lunchtime, Tiffany texted him to ask if Lacy had gone. He gave his ex the answer he knew would please her then did a double take when her BMW approached the barn.

What the hell?

"I had to be sure she wasn't here." Tiffany slammed her car door. "The bitch took out a temporary restraining order on me. We'll get that cleared up at the hearing."

Johnny had forgotten about it and dipped his head to hide his smirk. "You come to pick Nick up?"

"Yeah, and I wanted to see you." She straddled one of his legs with hers and pressed her hips into his thigh. "We never got to finish what we started last weekend." She squeezed his butt, and his body betrayed him.

Son of a gun. "Aren't you back together with Todd?"

"So?" One corner of her mouth twitched.

"I don't think he'd like it if he knew you were here, and this was about to happen." It was his turn to press into her a little.

"Todd's great and all, built to handle, but *this* is what I'm here for." She stroked him through his jeans. "I've missed you, Johnny. You always knew how to rock my world. And if I remember right, I could rock yours, too."

He stumbled away and made it inside the barn

before she cornered him and fumbled with his zipper.

"Mama D's at the house." Johnny reached for her hands.

"She can't see us." Tiffany slapped his hand away.

His damn dick kept getting harder the more she struggled with his belt. He wasn't going to get saved by the bell this time. Unless he restrained her more forcefully, she'd never stop until she got what she wanted. He needed to keep her happy, so she wouldn't sue someone and make all their lives hell, but he couldn't let this happen. Especially not with his feelings for Lacy. Just as she slid his zipper down, he lost his wood.

He placed his hands on Tiffany's shoulders, intending to push her away.

"Dad."

Johnny turned his back to the door to zip up and re-buckle his belt.

"Mama, what are you doing here?"

Nick looked upset, and Johnny bent to him. "Why are you home so early, bud?"

"I forgot it's an early release day since it's Halloween. We're going trick-or-treating in Atlanta. Right, Mama?" His hopeful expression tugged at Johnny's heart.

"That's right. Go get your things and we'll go."

Nick left and Tiffany patted Johnny's butt.

"Next time, we finish this." Her gaze roamed down to his crotch. "Unless you want to try for a quickie before he gets back."

"Better not. He'll be here in a flash." Johnny

stepped outside and went to her car to open the door for her. "Have fun trick-or-treating. I'll see you Sunday night."

Chapter Twenty

Lacy had never been to the coast of Georgia, but it was better than she imagined. She'd heard it was mostly marsh, but the little place called Quiet Cove had been built up with sand. It was more like the coastal islands, but technically was a peninsula.

She had fun playing with Ethan and taking care of the babies. They were so cuddly, and when they smiled and cooed at her, she thought her heart might sing with joy.

"Are all babies so sweet?" she asked Jane and Liz on Friday after lunch.

"All of the Baker babies are sweet." Liz winked. "I think it helps when you love kids, which you clearly do. You'll make a great mom someday, Lacy."

"Ha, thanks. If the day ever comes, I'll try to remember that."

"I was never around kids until I met the Bakers," Jane said. "I fell for Tyler and Ethan, and *all* of them. Now my own babies. They are the most precious things. Imagine getting to shape a life."

"Um, I don't want to think about that. I'm afraid I'll screw it up," Lacy admitted.

"You have so much love to give, there's no way you can screw that up," Liz said.

The door opened, and Danny came in with a man who looked familiar. Danny hugged his wife and dipped her back to kiss her, then picked up both babies at once to give them love.

The man, who resembled Danny, hugged and kissed Jane and Liz on their cheeks before he plucked Dillon from one of Danny's arms. Maybe this was a Baker she hadn't heard about.

"Lacy, this is our friend Breck Stanton."

She blinked about five times to clear her vision. He did look like the movie star with the same name. *Was she really meeting a real, live Hollywood icon?*

"Hi, Lacy." He extended his hand. "It's nice to meet you."

She shook his hand and tried to cover her star-struck stiffness. "Um, nice to meet you, too."

"She has that Southern accent. You should've warned me. I'm a sucker for a beautiful woman with a Southern accent." His blindingly white teeth seared her retinas.

She furrowed her brows at the same time she squinted from the glare. He was trying too hard to be nice, and it made him seem fake. Most women would probably fall and worship at his feet. If he expected her to, he was going to have to get a better line.

"Lacy, would you take Ethan up for a nap?" Liz kissed the boy all over his cheeks before she passed him to Lacy. "We need you rested before we trick-or-treat in a little while, sweet cheeks."

As Lacy climbed the stairs, she heard Danny say, "Don't even think about it, Breck. She's off limits."

She smiled to herself, flattered they thought a movie star might find her the least bit interesting. If they knew she'd grown up being called *trailer trash*, they'd think again.

Long after Ethan went to sleep in his toddler bed, which was shaped like a boat, she stayed in his room. The idea of going back downstairs or anywhere near Breck Stanton made her anxious.

Contemplating a nap, she leaned back in the recliner next to Ethan and wondered what Johnny was up to.

***

When Johnny arrived at Danny's house, it was late afternoon. They were expecting him, but he wasn't expecting Breck. Immediately, he worried Lacy had succumbed to his Hollywood good looks.

Johnny tried to play it off by making small talk for a few minutes, until he couldn't stand it any longer. "Where's Lacy?"

"She took Ethan up a little while ago and hasn't come back down," Liz said.

Johnny mounted the stairs in search of her and found her snoozing in the chair in Ethan's room.

He squatted beside the recliner. "When I told you to pretend to work, I didn't think you'd actually do it."

She opened her eyes, a smile spreading across her pretty face. He didn't let her get up on her own. Instead, he picked her up and held her close.

"Did you miss me?" he asked.

"Yes." She hugged him tight. "How's Nick?"

"Fine, I'll tell you all about it. Let's get out of here, so we don't wake the little man."

"If Jane doesn't need me, we can walk on the beach, if you want." She held onto his hand as he led her down the stairs.

"You like it down here?"

"Yeah, but just to visit. I wouldn't want to live here. There's sand everywhere. Impossible to keep clean."

He pulled her past the family gathered in the living room. "Going for a walk. Be back soon."

"Gosh, don't drag her, you caveman," Liz said. "And don't be long, we're going out after Ethan hits a few houses."

"What does she mean? Where are we going?" Lacy asked.

"Something about a costume party. She doesn't get out much. She's going to borrow your Stormtrooper stuff, and Breck's using my Darth Vader gear, so they won't be recognized."

"Do I have to go?"

"I'm afraid she'll insist. She doesn't want it to feel like she and Breck are on a date. They're just friends. She wants it to be a group outing."

"Is that why you came down here?"

"No, I came because I can't stand being apart from you."

"Stop it." She swatted his arm with her free

hand.

"Stop what? Telling the truth? I can't help how I feel about you, Lacy. If you don't return my affection, then please tell me." He turned to face her.

"It's not that Johnny, it's just—"

"So you do like me? Just a little bit, Little Bit?" He held up his hand and put about an inch distance between his thumb and forefinger.

She touched her thumb and forefinger together and put it inside his before forcing them further apart. "More than a little bit."

With the encouragement, he kissed her, and she kissed him back. His arms encircled her waist, and her hands rested on his shoulders. This was how it was supposed to be—a perfect fit, a perfect kiss, his perfect woman.

They stood, lip-locked, for a long time before he came up for air. He put a little distance between them, so she wouldn't be able to feel exactly how happy he was.

A little kid yelled, "Miw Wady," and they turned to see Ethan running toward them.

Lacy bent down and scooped him up into her arms.

"Hey, bud." Johnny ruffled his hair. "I know she's a lot prettier than me, but Uncle Johnny needs a hug, too."

"Wunka Wohnny." Ethan reached his arms out, and Johnny took him.

Liz joined them. "Sorry for the interruption, but we need to get Lacy ready."

"Ready for what?" Her eyes went wide.

"You're going to be Princess Leia this evening, my dear," she said.

"No, Liz. You guys go without me. I'll stay with the kids."

Liz shook her head. "We have another babysitter coming. Sorry, girlfriend, but you're going out tonight. You're gonna look great, and you're gonna have fun whether you like it or not."

They started walking back toward the house, Liz dragging Lacy in her wake.

"Wing, Miw Wady," Ethan said.

"Oh, you don't want to hear me sing, little man," Lacy said.

"Yes, he does," Johnny said. "It would be a nice reward for my traveling all the way here to see you."

She twisted her lips and pointed a sharp finger at him. "Not in front of anyone, but you three."

Johnny's heart was lighter than it had been in a long time. He'd won a small victory in his quest for Lacy to let him into her life, and hopefully, her heart.

***

Lacy sat as still as possible while Liz did her hair and makeup. Since she was a lot shorter than Liz, they'd gotten Lacy a costume in her size.

"I feel like I have cinnamon rolls on the side of my head," Lacy complained.

"I'll tell Johnny not to eat your hair," Liz said.

Lacy giggled. "You guys tease him a lot."

"Yeah, that's what siblings are for. He can take it. Lord knows he can dish it out better than most."

Lacy was still having a moral dilemma about

kissing Johnny and telling him she liked him. She more than liked him, but she loved her job and was afraid of losing everything. She'd never had so much to lose.

They went downstairs to find the guys waiting for them. Johnny wore the Han Solo costume, and he looked darn good. Lacy tried not to stare at the open neck, where just a little chest hair peeked out, the chest she dreamed of resting her head on.

Hot-to-mighty.

"Okay, Johnny, will you and Lacy take Ethan up to the doors? I'll drive," Liz said. "We'll be half an hour at the most."

"Don't you want to see him say 'trick or treat'?" Lacy asked.

"Yes, but I'm afraid…of being recognized." Liz explained who Ethan's father was and why privacy and anonymity were so important to her.

"Wear the mask," Lacy said. "No one will be able to see who you are."

Ethan wore his Yoda costume and was escorted by his mom and uncle to the doors of about five houses. That was all it took for his little pumpkin basket to get filled up. Lacy walked with them and took Ethan's picture with one of Jane's cameras.

The babysitter was waiting when they got back to the house, and they all loaded in one SUV to go to the costume party. All couples were stopped at the door to have their picture taken.

Liz and Breck accompanied each other and kept their masks in place for the photos, blaster and lightsaber poised for action. Danny and Jane were next, dressed as Padmé and Anakin. Lacy and

Johnny were last, and just before the photographer snapped their picture, Johnny laid her back and kissed her. Their picture was undoubtedly the best. And Lacy's heart would not stop thumping against her ribs.

"I want a copy of that." Johnny got the photographer's contact information.

He took her hand and led her through the crowd to where his family had found a table.

"What are you drinking, Lacy?" Danny asked.

"Um, Diet Coke."

"Aw, come on," Breck said. "You have to drink alcohol. That's half the point of adult costume parties."

"I don't drink alcohol, but knock yourself out."

When Danny and Breck left to go to the bar, Johnny turned to her. "Have you ever had alcohol before?"

"No."

"Because of your mom?"

She looked into his eyes and nodded. He understood her better than she realized.

"You guys should dance." Liz pushed Johnny's arm.

"You know I have two left feet sister," Johnny said. "And from what Nick tells me, Lacy is afflicted like me."

"It's a slow song, brother. All you have to do is sway side to side."

Danny and Breck returned with the drinks. Everyone had a beer, except Lacy. This was another reason she never went to bars. She was always the odd one.

"And here's your virgin, diet Cuba Libre." Breck winked. "It sounds better than Diet Coke, doesn't it?"

As Johnny tensed beside her, she faked a smile. Breck's flirtatious behavior was going over as well with Johnny as it was with her.

She took Johnny's arm. "How 'bout that dance?"

He followed her onto the dance floor. "I don't know Breck very well, and he's always been nice to my family, but he's annoying me."

"Me too. This whole scene annoys me."

Johnny pulled back and looked at her. "Why didn't you say something?"

"I did. But apparently, your sister isn't used to anyone telling her no. I think she wanted to make me over or something."

"Come on. We're out of here." He pulled her toward the exit.

"Aren't we going to tell them we're leaving?" She glanced over her shoulder as her feet moved forward.

"Nope. I'll text them later."

"Can I go change out of this costume?" she asked.

"Absolutely. I never understood the appeal of the Leia hair buns. Looks like a pastry stuck on the side of your head."

Lacy laughed. "That's what I said." She began pulling bobby pins from her hair.

"Do you want to walk or get a cab?" he asked.

"Walking's fine with me."

They took their boots off and walked in the

sand. They passed a giant bonfire where there was another costume party in progress—mostly pirates and mermaids.

"The beach is crowded," she said.

"So much for a romantic, moonlit stroll." He wriggled his eyebrows.

"I don't care about that," she said.

"I thought all women wanted romance."

Lacy hesitated before she spoke. She wanted to tell Johnny something about herself, but she wasn't sure how. "I'd just settle for not getting beat up."

He stopped and turned to place a hand on her cheek. "You deserve so much better, Lacy."

"There was a time when I didn't believe that." She held his gaze.

"What made you change your mind?"

She looked down. "Waking up in the hospital and realizing that if something didn't change, one day I wouldn't wake up."

He took her hands in his. "I'm sorry you had to spend even one second in fear for your safety—for your life. I don't want you to ever have to feel that way again. You're safe with me. You know that, right?"

"I know you'd never hurt me." She reached up and ran her fingers down his cheek. "You're a good man."

She was about to stand on tippytoes and kiss him when his phone rang.

"Darn phones. Hold that thought." He reached into his pocket and stepped away to answer the call.

When he hung up, he cussed a blue streak. "I'm sorry, I have to get back home. Nick fell while trick-or-treating and broke his arm."

"Oh, my God." She clutched her hand to her chest. "Is there anything I can do?"

"Can you run?"

Chapter Twenty-one

Johnny thought he might bust a gut from the run back to Danny's house. He called his brother to fill him in and the pilot to see how fast he could get to Atlanta.

Lacy changed and waited for him to pack. Telling her goodbye this time was more difficult than the last. He gave her a long kiss and a hug before he hauled himself away.

Wringing his hands, he paced the narrow aisle of the jet. *Poor Nick.* Johnny ought not be surprised at his son having his first break, but he wished he'd been there with him. Nick must've been so afraid.

When Johnny arrived after midnight, Mama D and Big Daddy were both at the hospital with Tiffany and Nick.

"He's all right." Mama D called on her nursing background to reassure him.

"It's kinda like that time Paul broke his arm when y'all were wrestling, and he took a spill down the stairs," his dad said.

"Now I know how upset you must've been." Johnny hugged his dad.

"Boys will be boys." Big Daddy grinned. "It was bound to happen sooner or later, but I admit I was a little bit terrified in the beginning."

"Johnny, I'm really sorry." Tiffany hugged him and rubbed his chest. "He was with a big group of kids, and it was dark. He just didn't know he was stepping off a ledge."

Johnny tried to keep the accusatory tone out of his voice. "Did you see it happen?"

"No, I was at home. He went with some of the neighbor kids."

"What adult was with them?" Johnny asked.

Her lips formed a tight line. "They're old enough not to need an adult holding their hand every second."

As he took a step back, Johnny inhaled deeply and let it out slowly. "I know what happened was an accident, but he's seven. He's not old enough to be unchaperoned."

"Daddy."

Johnny went to Nick's bedside. "Hey, buddy. How are you feeling?"

"I got a cast, and my friends at school can write their names on it."

"You bet. I can sign it too, right? Or is it uncool for your dad to sign your cast?" Johnny crossed his eyes.

"You can sign it. If Miss Lacy was here, she could sign it, too."

Johnny prayed Tiffany would keep her mouth

shut, and for once, she did.

"Tell me you at least got a ton of candy before you fell."

"I got half a bag, but that's enough. Miss Lacy says too much candy will rot my teeth and give me a bellyache."

"Aunt May used to say the same thing to me when I was your age." He kissed Nick's forehead.

"He keeps going on about her as if he expects her to come back," Tiffany said. "But that's not going to happen. You guys should go ahead and tell him the truth."

"Dad?"

"Get some rest, Nick-Nock. We'll talk tomorrow." Johnny bent to whisper in his ear. "Don't forget who loves you, baby."

Once Johnny's parents left, he took a chair next to the bed, and Tiffany took one on the other side. He dozed off and had a dream about Lacy singing to him. It took an erotic turn, and he woke up coming—in his ex-wife's mouth. His body stiffened as a key body part decidedly softened.

She swallowed and wiped her lips. "Good morning, stud."

Johnny glanced over at Nick who quickly shut his eyes. Johnny wondered how much of that his son had seen. He stood and grabbed Tiffany by the arm, dragging her to the bathroom.

"Is it my turn now, big boy?"

He'd never wanted to hit a woman before, but in that moment, it seemed justified. Thinking of Lacy made him back down.

"If you ever do anything like that in front of

my son again, I *will* make you regret it." His teeth were clenched, his voice a growl.

"What? He was asleep."

"No. He wasn't. Your behavior has become increasingly disturbing. I never questioned your ability to parent our son until now. You get your shit together, or I'll take him away from you. Do you understand what I'm saying?" His grip on her arms grew tighter as he spoke.

"Ow." She yanked out of his grasp and shoved at him. "God, Johnny, it's not like I murdered somebody. What's your fucking problem?"

They continued to argue until they heard a voice on the other side of the door.

***

Lacy's cell phone woke her up early on Saturday. "Hey, Johnny. How's Nick?"

"It's me, Miss Lacy. I miss you."

She sat up. "I miss you too, sweetie. How's your arm?"

He told her about having surgery and the cast and people signing it for him.

"Is your dad there?" she asked.

"He's in the bathroom with Mommy. They're having sex."

Lacy choked on her own spit. "They're what?"

"Yeah, Mama was licking Dad's ding-a-ling, and then he took her in the bathroom. You know. Sex."

Lacy's stomach burned, and she darted to her own bathroom to wretch. He'd just been kissing her the night before, and now he was having sex with Tiffany.

Sitting back on her haunches, she put the phone to her ear again. “Nick, I don’t think you were meant to see that. I’m really sorry. You probably shouldn’t mention it to your dad and don’t tell him you called me. Your mama isn’t a fan of mine. I have to go, but I love you, and I miss you like crazy. Don’t forget, okay?”

“Okay, Miss Lacy. I love you, too.”

Lacy put the phone down and rubbed her forehead hard just to be sure she was awake. What she’d just heard wasn’t her worst nightmare, but it was still painful.

Tears ran in streaks down her face for the fool she’d been to believe Johnny could really care about someone like her. She reminded herself who she really was—bottom of the barrel trailer trash. It was what she’d been her whole life and nothing would change.

She might as well go back to North Carolina and wait for Stan to get paroled, so he could beat her to death and put her out of her misery. She thought she’d come so far, but it had been an illusion, a lie she was telling herself.

When she heard the twins cry, she was already showered and dressed. In the nursery, she changed one diaper, then the next.

“Let’s get some grub, kiddos.” She picked up one baby in one arm and then the other.

Turning toward the door, she nearly shrieked at Breck who stood in the doorway, shirtless. Her eyes were full for a few seconds as she realized why they paid him the big bucks. It was shocking to see so many muscles in one place.

"You're good with kids," he said.

"Thanks. Here, make yourself useful." She handed him a baby.

He followed her downstairs, where she made bottles and put cereal in them like Jane had taught her.

"You like working for the Bakers?" he asked.

She froze and looked at him across the kitchen island. "Why? Do you know someone who needs a live-in nanny and housekeeper?"

"You looking?"

She glanced toward the hallway before she spoke. "Yes."

"Why?" He narrowed his dark eyes at her. "I thought you and Johnny were hot and heavy."

She twisted her mouth. "That's not gonna work out. His ex-wife is back in his bed…I mean life." *Shoot*. She hadn't meant to give that away.

His eyebrows shot up. "You're kidding?"

A door closed somewhere in the house.

"Quick, do you know of anyone or not?" she asked.

"I'll ask around. You willing to move to L.A.?"

"I'll go wherever the work is, and don't say anything to them yet. Please." She pleaded with her eyes.

"Your secret's safe with me." He put the empty bottle on the counter. "This kid's farting all over me."

"This one, too." She held the baby up and spoke to her. "Baby farts are cute, unless they're wet. Right, Dillon?"

"That's so gross." Breck aimed Davis's butt

away from him.

"Are you calling my kid gross?" Jane asked as she joined them. "Thank you guys so much. Danny detained me this morning when he heard you were up, Lacy."

"TMI," Breck said and passed Davis to her.

"Agreed," Lacy added.

"Have you spoken to Johnny?" Jane asked.

Lacy opened her eyes wide, so the tears brimming wouldn't overflow. Why was she crying again? She shook her head because she was afraid to speak with the lump in her throat.

Danny strolled in. "Hey, anyone talk to Johnny? I was about to call him."

Lacy gave a quick shake of her head as she passed Dillon to Danny then headed toward the stairs to check on Ethan and Liz.

"Wait, Lace," Danny said. "Johnny may want to talk to you."

"Not if Tiffany's there." She kept going.

When she came back down a few minutes later with Ethan on her hip, Danny studied her. "You were right. She was there. Nick's fine. He'll be in a cast for a while."

Lacy put Ethan in a highchair and made his breakfast. She was still having trouble believing who his dad was. Talk about living with a big secret.

Despite her aching heart, she was hopeful after talking to Breck. There were so many opportunities for her out there; she never had to go back to what she was before.

While she stirred and blew on Ethan's oatmeal,

she looked up to see Breck watching her.

"Be patient," she said. "You're next."

Chapter Twenty-two

On Saturday, after Johnny returned to Southland with Nick, he called Lacy's cell phone. When she didn't answer, he left a message then leaned back to watch some Southeastern Conference football.

Nick was asleep on the sofa with his feet in Johnny's lap. Johnny absently rubbed Nick's lower legs and glanced at his phone every other minute.

He called her again. No answer.

She was probably busy babysitting the kids since Danny, Jane, Liz, and Breck were going to the game. When he remembered Breck was there, Johnny groaned inwardly. At least Lacy hadn't seemed overly impressed by the famous Adonis.

Returning his focus to football, Johnny relaxed his shoulders. There was a time when he would've moved heaven and earth to be in Jacksonville on Halloween weekend for the *World's Largest Cocktail Party* and see the game in person. But his priorities had shifted drastically over the last few months. Nick was his number one, and he'd do whatever it took to keep his son safe and sound.

A half hour later, he tried again and left another voicemail. He was desperate to hear her voice, so he called his brother.

Danny answered, but the background noise made it hard to hear.

"Hey, bro. Lacy's not answering her phone."

"We just got into the stadium, and the ladies are doing the group bathroom thing," Danny spoke loudly. "I don't know if she has her phone, but she probably couldn't hear you anyway. Let me call you later."

"Just tell her I'm home and to call me when she can." He huffed out a breath.

Lacy had never been to a Georgia game. He hadn't expected her to go. Resentment rested in the muscles of his neck. He wanted to experience it with her. Be there to see her reaction to the crowds and the excitement. Hold her hand.

If she'd been unhappy at the bar the night before, she would've hated the tailgate party. He wanted to know more about her and her past, but now that she was ready to let him in, they were forced to be apart. His disdain toward Tiffany grew more with each passing moment.

Big Daddy came in and handed Johnny a beer before he sat in his recliner. Shaking off his melancholy, Johnny turned to his father for advice.

Scooting closer, he spoke quietly. "Dad, can I talk to you about something?"

He told his dad about his problems with his ex-wife, including the oral sex in front of Nick.

"I hate to say this, son, because it might mean war, but you should call Nancy. Nick shouldn't have to be exposed to Tiffany's behavior. It's your job to protect him, but you know that." His dad sipped his beer. "I think you know what you need to do, but you're afraid of the battle that's coming. I'll be right beside you."

Johnny ran his hand through his hair and let out a sigh. "All right, I'll put on my armor and call Nancy. Then we'll watch some Georgia football."

Before he stepped outside with his phone, he bent to kiss Nick's head and prayed he was doing the right thing.

***

Lacy checked her cell when they got back to the house. She'd left it behind for two reasons. One, it was her work phone, and it didn't feel right taking it to a football game. And two, she didn't want to talk to Johnny…except she did. She wanted to tell him about all the drunk idiots at the football game who scared and entertained her at the same time.

It would've been easy to lean on Breck, since he'd offered to protect her, but she'd made it a point to keep someone between them, even more someones when the cameras found him in the crowd and put him on the big screen. At the time, both Lacy and Liz were scrambling to see who could get further away from the movie star.

Breck had held up his UGA ball cap, and the entire place starting doing the whooping dog bark thing Nick had taught her. Thinking of him made her desperate to check on him. Worry for the sweet boy had niggled at her all day.

When she looked at her phone, there were two voicemails from Johnny. The first one updated her on Nick's condition. The second said how much he missed her.

"Liar," she said to the phone as she deleted the message.

"Talking to yourself?" Breck asked from the open door to her room.

"Yeah. No. I'm a coward." She tossed the phone onto the bed behind her and gripped her head with both hands. "I guess I need to talk to him, but I'd rather not."

Breck came into the room and sat next to her. "Do you want to practice on me? You can tell me off and plan what you want to say. Are you sure about your information?"

"That's the problem. I can't reveal my source, so I need to show disinterest, I guess." She shrugged. "I don't know what to do, but I hate lying."

"Want some advice from an award-winning actor?" His thousand-watt smile nearly blinded her.

"You are so full of yourself." She looked away, unable to believe she'd said those words out loud to the world-famous Breck Stanton.

He chuckled. "I need friends like you to keep me humble. I want to help, if you'll let me."

"You gonna pretend to be my boyfriend?" Lacy laughed as soon as she said it, knowing she'd never pull it off.

"I hadn't thought of that, but it's an angle we can try. I'd be proud to be your boyfriend. You're cute as a button. I could put you in my back pocket and take you back to L.A. with me."

"No wonder your initials are BS. Completely full of it." She shook her head. "Do you know how insincere you sound when you say things like that?"

"Seriously? People in my business like having their butts kissed. I must be losing my touch." He puckered his lips. "I'm sorry, but sometimes I don't know how to act around regular people. Not that being regular is a bad thing." He nudged her with his elbow, which was probably insured for forty million dollars.

"The effusive compliments make it seem like you're trying too hard. Just relax, you don't have to tell everyone how great they are. Especially when they're not used to hearing it."

"You need to be told every day." He grinned.

"Now, you're just flirting," Lacy said.

"He does that." Jane stood in the open doorway. "He'll try to charm your pants off."

"Spoken like someone who's been there," Lacy said.

The look Jane shot her was scary, but Breck laughed. Lacy had hit a nerve.

Her face heated. "Sorry, I had no idea."

"That's why it's so funny." Breck bounced beside her.

"Breck, do you want to get out of Lacy's bedroom? Johnny would not be happy." Jane crossed her arms over her chest.

Lacy put her arm out to stop Breck from getting up. "He's helping me with a problem concerning Johnny, and we haven't worked it out yet."

Jane raised an eyebrow. "Can I help?"

Lacy looked at Breck who shrugged. Lacy twisted her lips. It was strange how she noticed when she did that now. If Johnny were here, he'd tell her to say what was on her mind.

She sighed. "Can I talk to all of you together?"

They gathered around the bar in the kitchen, and Lacy told them what Nick said when he'd called her that morning.

"No way," Danny said then called Johnny.

A few moments of mumbling passed. "Shit." Danny covered the phone with his hand. "It's true. Lacy, he wants to talk to you."

***

Johnny looked skyward and whispered a quick prayer. "Let her hear me out." He waited long seconds before she came on the line.

"Hello." Her voice was shaky.

"Is my family staring at you?"

"Yes."

"Can you walk outside or to another room?"

"Okay."

"What did Nick say exactly?"

"I'm not comfortable repeating it. Would *you* have told me if he hadn't?"

"No."

"That's what I thought." The line went dead.

A moment later his phone rang. "Johnny, what the hell are you doing?" Danny asked. "Lacy's upset. And for good reason."

He sighed. "It's a misunderstanding."

Johnny explained the best he could and told his

brother about his decision to fight for full custody of Nick.

"What are you going to do about Lacy?" Danny asked.

"She never should've found out. She'll probably never listen to me, and I guess I deserve that. I should have dealt with Tiffany directly, instead of dancing around the issues. It was another dumb move. Classic Johnny." He hit himself in the forehead with the heel of his hand.

"Don't be so hard on yourself, little brother. And give Lacy some time; she may come around. She must care about you, or she wouldn't feel so hurt."

"I promised I'd never hurt her. But I was so focused on one kind of hurt, I never thought about the other." Johnny closed his eyes.

After tossing his phone on the bedside table, he dropped his head in his hands. Nick was already in bed, but tomorrow, they'd need to talk about sex and what he'd seen.

Lying on the bed, Johnny wished he hadn't blown his chance with Lacy. He was tired of always being a screw-up. For once, he wanted to do something right. Maybe, in time, she could forgive him.

With a custody contest in his future, he needed to focus. It wouldn't be easy forcing Lacy out of his head or his heart, so it was a good thing she wasn't at Southland to distract him.

A gnawing feeling ate at his insides. He couldn't let her go. She was the one. He could feel it in his bones, but he'd probably never get to tell her.

Unable to give up on her completely, he resigned himself to postponing his pursuit.

***

Lacy cried herself to sleep for the first time in a long while. Was it asking too much to want a man who would respect her physically and emotionally?

Breck shook her awake the next morning. He was nice to wake up to, like a dream. As he stood by her bed, she blinked a few times to be sure he was real.

“Let’s go for a run before everyone else gets up,” he said.

“Why do you hate me?” She pulled the covers up and turned over.

“Come on. It’s a great way to burn off some steam.” He bounced the mattress.

“I’ve got plenty of that.” She rolled out of bed and found something to wear.

They ran barefoot on the sand, and within a few minutes, her feet cramped. “I’m dying.”

“You’re a wimpy little thing, aren’t you?” He smirked.

She pointed a finger at him. “You sassing me, boy?”

“Yep.” He picked her up, threw her over his shoulder, and kept running.

She held in a squeal and tried to brace herself. “Nice butt. It’d be better if my face wasn’t smacking into it every other step.”

“You’re going to complain one way or the other, aren’t you?” He slowed to a walk.

“I’ll try to run and not fuss. I promise.”

When he set her back on her feet, she ran, albeit slowly. But it was a start.

As he jogged beside her, he turned his head her way. “I wasn’t kidding when I said I’d put you in my back pocket and take you home with me.”

“I’ve been in your back pocket, and it’s not as fun as people might think.” She fought a smile.

“You know how to keep me grounded, Lacy. I like that.”

“I like the way my name sounds on your lips.” She didn’t know why she was flirting with Breck Stanton, except that since she’d woken up, she hadn’t thought about Johnny—until now. *Dammit.*

“Oh, now you want to play?” He pursed his lips. They were pretty lips.

“I’m sorry.” She shrugged one shoulder. “I was just having fun.”

“You could use more fun in your life. You seem kind of uptight.”

She nodded. “I’m a mess.”

“A hot mess.”

“And I can’t breathe.” She slowed to walk and catch her breath. “You suck, Breck. Whoever said you were the cat’s meow lied.”

“Ouch, woman. I think you’re taking out your frustration with Johnny on me. You should try keeping it pent up inside.” He patted his chest. “Let it fester.”

She stopped and faced him. He stepped closer, and she stood on tippytoes and kissed him. Didn’t even hesitate.

How many chances in your life do you get to kiss a movie star?

When she broke the kiss, he looked stunned. His mouth hung open, and his hands held the empty air where she'd just been. "I wasn't ready. Do that again."

She turned and jogged down the beach, proud of herself for her tramp-like behavior. Maybe she should get a tramp stamp to commemorate the event.

Soon, her shoulders slumped because no one had ever kissed her like Johnny. His kisses made her feel like the most important person in the world. But then again, they probably made Tiffany feel that way, too.

Chapter Twenty-three

Legal hell. There was such a place, and Johnny was in it. He remembered why he never tried for full custody in the first place. He was no saint.

In his life, he'd made a lot of dumb mistakes, and Tiffany's lawyer was bringing them all back to bite him in the ass. All the way back to the magic mushroom tea he drank in high school before trying to fly off the top of the bleachers, to the more recent incident where his insane girlfriend pulled a gun on him because he wasn't his brother.

Tiffany had known Johnny most of his life, so she had all the dirt, and unfortunately, she wasn't afraid to use it.

"You need to look really stable, Johnny," Nancy said. "Settled. Serious relationship. Married would be best."

"How do you suggest I accomplish that, Aunt Nancy? What idiot would marry me to help me get custody of my son?" He rested his head on the dining table.

"I can think of one," Mama D said. "But she's not an idiot."

"Would she?" His dad's voice held a note of hope.

Johnny lifted his eyes to his parents who were seated across from him.

He shook his head. "No, she wouldn't. She's pissed at me over what happened with Tiffany."

"The custody hearing is scheduled for January. We need to get you married and stable by Thanksgiving." Nancy tapped the legal pad in front of her.

"I can't ask her to do that." Johnny rubbed his eyes with the heels of his hands.

"But we can," Mama D said. "She loves Nick. She'll do it."

"No." He banged his fist down so hard the table vibrated. "There has to be another way. I won't do it. I won't ask her to."

"Do you think she'd be a suitable mother for Nick?" Nancy wrote on her notepad.

"Absolutely. But I could never ask her to pretend to love me for his sake." Johnny closed his eyes, wishing they would leave it alone. Couldn't they see he loved her too much to ask her to participate in a lie of epic proportions?

"She'd do it for Nick." His dad shifted in his seat, the chair screeching on the pine floors. "And we could throw in a payoff, once the custody issue is settled."

"No, Dad." Johnny reached his hand across the expanse of oak, pleading with them. "A payoff will insult her. She's not like Tiffany. Please, I'm asking you to help me find another way. I've changed. Y'all know I have. But there's much more evidence of the man I was than the man I am."

"We'll help you, honey. Leave it to us." Mama D patted his hand.

***

The Sunday before Thanksgiving, Lacy rubbed her eyes to be sure she wasn't hallucinating. Mr. and Mrs. Baker had arrived at the beach, earlier than expected.

Mrs. Baker took Dillon from her arms and kissed the baby before she hugged Lacy.

"When will Nick and Johnny get here?" Lacy asked, dreading the answer. It would be great seeing Nick, but awkward being around his dad.

"They'll fly in Wednesday. We came early to help shop and cook and tell you how much we've missed you." Mr. Baker gave her a side hug.

Lacy almost bought their story, but like Breck and his insincerity, the Bakers' attention felt forced. Not something she'd ever experienced with them before.

Later that night, they revealed their real reason for coming early. She clenched her teeth and sucked spit between them. It was a new thing she did when she thought of Johnny. It kept her from crying. The elder Bakers explained the details of their plan.

"Johnny's too proud to ask you for help." Mrs. Baker sat next to her on a barstool.

"Why? He wasn't too proud to…never mind." Her voice trailed off.

"He was asleep," Mr. Baker said. "That was all

Tiffany's doing. He said he was dreaming about you."

"Is it supposed to make me feel better to know that while Tiffany had her mouth on him, he was thinking of me?" She crossed her arms over her chest, embarrassed to talk about oral sex with Johnny's father.

"Lacy, please. For Nick's sake, we need you," Mr. Baker said.

"Are you telling me that if I marry Johnny, then he can get full custody of Nick?" Lacy asked.

"Yes. At least, his chances will be much better," Mama D said. "And we'll pay you, and you can get a divorce in six months or a year, whatever suits you. You'll have to sign a pre-nuptial agreement, of course."

"You think I'd take money to protect Nick and give him a better life?" Lacy asked, her limbs growing heavier with the increase in her disappointment. Didn't they know her at all?

Liz unclenched her jaw. "Y'all, this is over the line. You can't expect her to agree to it. If you want to let her go, I'll keep her on as a nanny for Ethan."

Jane shook her head and put her hand on top of Lacy's. "We've got your back. No matter what decision you make, you have my support."

Lacy looked down, attempting to nod her thanks as she slid off her stool and went to her room.

Liz followed and hugged her. "I'm so sorry. I meant what I said. I'll hire you to keep my house, now that it's finished, and help me with Ethan. If you want to get away for a few days, say the word.

I'll send you on a holiday anywhere you want."

"That sounds British—holiday." Lacy covered her face with both of her hands and cried.

"I can't help it. He's in my soul." Liz wiped her eyes.

"I bet you're in his, too." Lacy sniffed. "I bet every time he hears a Southern accent, he thinks of you. Just like Johnny and Nick. They're in my soul, too." She'd never really admitted it to herself, much less out loud to anyone else. But somewhere along the way, she'd let Johnny slip past her self-imposed barriers and into her heart.

What if his kiss hadn't been a lie? What if he really cared about her? If he did, wouldn't he be the one proposing, instead of his parents?

"So, you'll do it?" Liz asked. "You're willing to live a lie to help my brother get custody of his son?"

Lacy didn't answer right away. If it would help Johnny and Nick, she'd do whatever the Bakers asked. She just wished they understood her better—knew she wouldn't take money for it.

She planned to call Nancy and include her own terms for the pre-nup. Two could play at this game.

***

The Saturday after Thanksgiving, instead of watching Georgia beat Georgia Tech, the Bakers watched Johnny exchange vows with Lacy.

During the ceremony, he silenced a groan. After his divorce from Tiffany, he swore the next time he got married, it would be for love. True love by *both parties*. So much for keeping promises to himself.

It was all a lie. Lacy didn't even look him in the eye when she said "I do." Tears ran down her cheeks the entire time, and he sucked up a few of his own.

More than once before the wedding, he'd tried to call it off. But everyone kept pushing him, telling him it was the right thing to do, including Lacy. Then, when he'd look at Nick's smiling face, he'd had no choice.

Without reading it, Johnny had signed the prenuptial agreement Nancy put in front of him. She'd guaranteed he could "afford" it. She even made air quotations with her fingers.

His family hated him, starting with Aunt Nancy all the way down to Paul. Or maybe he just hated himself for always being a fool.

The only person who was truly thrilled about the union was Nick. Since the moment of their arrival, if Nick wasn't playing with his cousins, he was clinging to Lacy. He hadn't done that to Tiffany since he was a toddler. His new stepmom definitely filled a void in his life.

Afterward, while his family had punch and cake, Johnny sat on the sand facing the Atlantic Ocean. In the late afternoon sun, with the rays dancing on the water, it was hard to imagine his life was all bad.

He was drinking from a long-neck bottle when his *wife* sat down beside him.

"That was the worst wedding of all time." She sipped a beer.

"Being married to me has turned you into a drinker already? I'm not sure it'll help my case."

"It's a root beer." She held up the bottle. "Don't worry. I'll try not to wreck your life."

"Like I've wrecked yours?" He played with the white gold band on his ring finger.

"I admit it wasn't the wedding I dreamed about. In my dream, I was seven months pregnant, and my dad was holding a shotgun." A tiny smile played at the corners of her lips.

"I guess my dad was holding a metaphorical shotgun today, also known as his checkbook." He let out a humorless laugh.

Turning away, she pressed her fist to her mouth. Before he could reach out to her, she sprang to her feet and walked away, never looking back.

He let her go.

That night, Johnny stared at the ceiling in Liz's new house, wondering if his bride was also suffering from insomnia, down the beach at Danny and Jane's place. Misery roiled in his stomach like the waves of the ocean outside his window.

Was there anything more pathetic than spending your wedding night alone?

Chapter Twenty-four

On Sunday, Lacy hugged Liz, Jane, and Danny and kissed their kids goodbye. She boarded Mr. Baker's plane and sat across the aisle from Nick, who hadn't been still in four days.

He bounced in his seat and spoke so fast she had trouble keeping up. "I can't wait to get back to Southland. Do you know why, Miss Lacy? My dad and I have a big surprise for you."

"Nick," Johnny said from his chair behind them. "You aren't supposed to ruin the surprise."

"He won't ruin anything." She patted her lap. "Come sit with me."

Nick did and leaned against her chest. She put her arms around him and rested her head back to look out of the small window.

If only Johnny would talk to her, it might help ease the ache in her belly. But he couldn't even stand to look at her. She didn't blame him. She'd never been valued by anyone—her mom, nor Stan, who'd claimed to love her. And now, her husband, who'd never claimed to be anything more than her friend didn't think much of her either.

When they started descending, she jolted awake. Nick was asleep in her arms.

"Do you want me to take him?" Johnny asked from the seat Nick had occupied earlier.

She nodded. "My legs are asleep."

"He's almost as big as you." Johnny scooped his son up like he was a feather.

"It won't be long, and he'll be as tall as you are." Lacy tried a small smile. She had to do something to break the ice—to try to get back to the friendly place where they'd once been.

Nick woke up when they landed, just in time to carry his own suitcase off of the airplane. Johnny took his and Lacy's luggage.

Trying to get the feeling back, Lacy massaged her thighs for a few minutes. When she stood to follow everyone off the plane, she promptly fell down, not noticing her feet were asleep until they failed her.

Johnny was at the door when she hit the deck. The luggage landed with a thud, and he came back for her.

"Man down." She laughed.

He helped her stand and held on to steady her. "First day with your new feet?"

"Something like that." She smiled and held onto his arm.

Picking her up, he carried her to the car. Excitement coursed through her, but it was quickly replaced with melancholy. Would her husband have carried her over any threshold if her lower half hadn't been numb?

Mr. Baker drove, and Mrs. Baker sat up front. Nick sat in the middle between Lacy and Johnny. Lacy's gaze was drawn to the pine forests, which had never provided a more fascinating distraction.

When they reached Southland, Mr. Baker drove past the entrance. Lacy held her breath, unsure of what to expect.

Nick squirmed in his seat. "You're gonna love it, Miss Lacy."

About a quarter mile past Southland, they turned onto a narrow lane. Johnny had once told her about the timber land he owned and farmed. This was it.

The hard packed dirt path snaked right then left, winding them around until they came to a clearing. The woods gave way to meadows with an occasional live oak dotting the landscape.

After the next turn, Lacy saw something. In the late afternoon sun, she squinted to be sure there was really a mobile home in the distance, a double-wide. It had an enclosed carport attached, and Bessie was parked inside next to two golf carts. Johnny's newer truck was parked outside of the covered area.

Her blood flowed like molasses through her veins. At least, that's how it seemed when her pulse pounded in her head, slow and rhythmic.

Had he bought a trailer? For her? She scratched her chin and looked at Johnny, who wasn't looking at her.

"Do you like it? We've got our very own house," Nick said, "because we're a family."

When they got out, Nick took Lacy's hand and pulled her. "I'll show you around."

Her brain scrambled like eggs. Nick's words made no sense, just like Johnny's actions. She thought she'd be going back to her cottage, so she could nurse her aching heart in private.

"Wait, Nick-Nock," Mr. Baker said. "Your dad has to carry her over the threshold. It's tradition."

Lacy's cheeks heated up, and her sluggish heart beat sped up too fast. She'd been told about Mrs. Baker's ability to see spirits and have premonitions of death, but no one had told her Mr. Baker was the mind reader in the family.

***

Johnny mumbled under his breath and picked Lacy up to carry her inside. "Get the door, Nick."

"You got us a house?" she asked.

"I was going to build here eventually. We had to get something pre-fab since this was kind of fast. The court-appointed social worker has already been out here."

Once inside, he put her down, so damn mad at himself he could barely think.

Nick took her hand and led her to the master bedroom. Johnny stayed in the living room, while Nick gave her the tour. The master bed and bath were on one end of the house. Three bedrooms and one bath were on the other end. The open concept kitchen, dining, and living areas were in the middle.

She stopped when they returned to where he waited. "This is very nice, Johnny."

"I have to keep my things in your bedroom, but I'll sleep in the room next to Nick," Johnny said when Nick had his head stuck in the refrigerator.

"You don't have to…" She looked down at her hands. "I mean, I don't need the bigger room."

Nick skipped to where they stood in the living room, holding a juice box in his hand. "Miss Lacy, I know why yours and Dad's bedroom is not close to mine. It's so you can have sex. Dad told me all about it."

Johnny dropped his head and covered his face with his hand. He knew that conversation would come back to haunt him. "Nick, do you have to repeat everything I say?"

Nick smiled. "You're smart, Daddy. Miss Lacy, are you a screamer?"

Lacy's eyes almost bugged out of her head.

"Dad said that sometimes when people have sex, they holler real loud. Not because it hurts, but because it feels good." He sipped his drink.

"Nick, I think you're making Miss Lacy uncomfortable. She isn't used to talking about this with you. It's not really an appropriate conversation to have."

Lacy sat down on the couch and tugged Nick to stand in front of her. "Your dad's right. I'm not comfortable with the topic, but it doesn't mean you can't talk to me about that or anything else. If I feel weird about it, I'll send you to your dad for answers because I don't want to tell you the wrong thing. Asking me if I'm a screamer is a very personal question. You should never ask a woman that. It's kinda disrespectful because sex is private."

"But now that you're married to my dad, you can have sex with him, right? Then you'll be happy and my dad, too."

Johnny sat next to Lacy and took one of Nick's hands. "Son, we *are* happy."

"No, you're not. Not like you were before Miss Lacy left to help Aunt Lizabelle." Big tears welled up in his eyes. "Did I do something wrong?"

Johnny pulled Nick into his arms. "Of course not, buddy. But remember when I talked to you about sex and… Oh, Lord. I don't think I can do this." He turned his head away and shook it.

"Nick," Lacy said. "When you first broke your arm and you called me and told me your mom and dad were having sex, that hurt my feelings. Not because you told me, but I thought your dad lied to me about something."

"About what?" Nick asked.

"About his feelings for me. He told me he liked me, but I thought you were telling me he was getting back together with your mom. I misunderstood and I'm really sorry. That was my fault."

"No. It was my fault," Johnny said. "I should've told you what I was trying to do, but it was a bad plan. I knew that, but I did it anyway. I'm sorry, Lacy. I never meant to hurt you. I thought I was protecting you by not telling you, but I was wrong. It only hurt you more, and I have to clarify we didn't have sex."

"It was just a blow job. Right, Dad?" Nick sucked juice through a straw.

Johnny closed his eyes as his blood pressure hit an all-time high.

Lacy shook with contained laughter. "Nick."

“Was that too personal?”

“Yes,” she said. “And vulgar. There’s really not a good name for it, so how about you not say that word again until you’re in college.”

Johnny held his palms up at Lacy’s look. “I didn’t know what else to call it. I panicked when I tried to explain. And I was asleep when it happened. I only woke up when…you know?”

“Organism.” Nick chased the straw with his mouth.

Lacy pressed her lips together. “I think it’s more dangerous to go around half-cocked—”

Johnny’s laugh burst from him before he could stop it.

Nick giggled half-heartedly. “What’s so funny, Daddy?”

“Your dad’s laughing because I said cock. It’s another name for boy parts. Blow jobs fall under the category of oral sex, so it would be better if you called it that. It’s not an organism, it’s an orgasm. Biologically, it helps make babies.”

“I didn’t get all technical with him,” Johnny said. “Do you think I should?”

She lifted her shoulders. “I’m sure there’s a book we can order online with cartoon drawings and kid-friendly explanations.”

“Nick, you can talk to us about this in private any time,” Johnny said. “But don’t talk about it in front of anyone else, especially not the social worker or your mom.”

“Or your friends at school,” Lacy added.

“Okay, Dad. And Miss Lacy, if I hear you scream, I’ll cover my ears.”

"Honey, if you hear me scream, it probably means I'm getting beat to death, so you should run." Her lips held a half smile, but there was truth in her words.

Needing to reassure her, Johnny leaned his shoulder into hers. "That's not going to happen here, Little Bit."

"I know." She smiled and put her free arm around Nick.

Johnny let himself breathe for the first time in several weeks. They were right where they were supposed to be. Together.

Chapter Twenty-five

Two weeks later, Lacy had Southland decorated for Christmas. All she had left to do was the house she shared with Johnny and Nick. It was Nick's first day home from school for Christmas Break, and they were going to shop for lights and decorations for the Blue Spruce Johnny had chosen for them from his Christmas tree farm.

Yes, Lacy Goodwin Baker was a farmer's wife.

She chortled. If it were a real marriage, she would be proud.

Johnny had already left for Southland, and Nick was eating breakfast at the little round table. Lacy went to make Nick's and Johnny's beds since she and Johnny still weren't sleeping together or even sharing a bed. Nick thought it was because of snoring. The truth was things were still awkward, and they were easing into it.

"Somebody's here," Nick yelled. "It's probably the social worker."

Going to the window, Lacy peered out of the blinds. A little rust-colored Datsun pickup stopped. Looking at it more closely, she realized it wasn't rust-colored; it was just rusted.

A man got out, and Lacy grew faint, almost wetting herself as the hair on the back of neck rose.

"Nick." She stumbled down the hall. "Don't open the door."

"Why not?" His hand was on the knob.

She locked the dead bolt and backed away from the door, pulling Nick with her.

She knelt down to be on his eye level. "Listen to me very carefully. Do exactly what I tell you, no matter what happens. Do you understand?"

He nodded, but his eyes widened with fear. That was good. He needed to be afraid.

"I want you to sneak out the back door and get to Southland as fast as you can." She gripped his arms for emphasis.

The man pounded on the front door, and Lacy swallowed down a squeak.

"Don't let him see you, and don't look back. Just go, okay?"

Nick nodded, and the pounding got louder. "I know you're in there, Lacy."

Lacy let Nick out the back door and slid her wedding ring off her finger. It would definitely get her killed sooner rather than later. Placing the ring in an empty coffee cup on the counter, she exhaled and tensed her arms to stop her hands from shaking.

When she opened the door and peeked out, Stan's back disappeared around the side of the house.

No! She ran to the back door and out to the side of the house, where she found them.

"Who's your little friend, Lacy?" Stan looked back and forth between them.

"Nobody. Just a friend's kid I'm babysitting since school's out." *Good. Her voice was steady.* "He was coming outside to look for some pine cones. Right, Nick?"

Nick nodded as Stan's hand gripped his shoulder.

"Don't you have a kiss for old Stan? It's been nearly four years since I've felt those sweet lips." His eyes raked over her.

Feeling exposed somehow, she fidgeted. "Come on in the house, and let Nick go." She could barely hear herself over the blood rushing in her ears.

"I don't think I will. You come here *now* and kiss me, woman." He pointed to the ground by his feet.

Lacy took a few steps and turned her body so her left foot was forward. She gave him a kiss he wasn't expecting when her knuckles made contact under his chin. His head jerked back as he staggered, and he let go of Nick.

"Run." Lacy gave Nick a push.

Before Nick could get out of reach, Stan shoved the boy into the side of the trailer, and Nick fell to the ground. He bent to pick Nick up, but Lacy jumped on Stan's back and wrapped her arm around his neck, the way she'd seen wrestlers do it.

He straightened and tried to shake her off.

"Run, Nick." She squeezed with all her

strength.

Nick crawled away, then stood and ran. The high-pitched whine from the electric engine of the golf cart made her relax her grip a little. As the sound faded, Stan slammed her into the side of the house. She didn't let go the first time, but by the third, her teeth were rattling, and she released her hold.

She fell on the ground in a heap, but she didn't stay there long. Stan grabbed her arm and dragged her to the front door.

"Get your keys. We're leaving before that boy calls the law." He slung her into the house.

Her keys were by the front door next to her purse, which contained her phone. She grabbed both as he yanked her out the door. He took her car keys and told her to get in. Apparently, Bessie was in better shape than the Datsun.

Her sister-in-law Jane was a combat expert and had advised Lacy to disable her assailant and get away. Because of her small size, if her attacker got their hands on her, she was in trouble. She debated running, but if she detained Stan, Johnny would show up, and she didn't want him to get hurt.

The moves she'd learned in kickboxing class might help, but Lacy took too long trying to decide. Because of her hesitation, Stan backhanded her and shoved her into the car.

Stars flashed in her head as he slammed the door.

***

When he heard Nick yelling for him, Johnny was in the loft of the barn. "Up here, son."

“Dad, come quick. There’s a bad man with Miss Lacy. She told me to run.”

Johnny thought he heard wrong until he caught sight of the blood flowing from a cut on Nick’s forehead. With his stomach in his throat, Johnny descended the ladder, jumping from the fourth rung and dropping to his knees in front of Nick.

“What happened? Did he hurt you?” Johnny ran his hands over Nick’s arms and legs.

“He squeezed my shoulder. Then Miss Lacy hit him, and he pushed me into the house. That’s how I hit my head.”

“I’ll kill the son of a—” He picked his son up and ran to the house, calling for his mama. “Bring the first aid kit.”

While she doctored Nick, he repeated the story. Johnny grabbed his dad’s Beretta Storm and two loaded magazines. He inserted one mag and chambered a round. Not bothering with the holster, he shoved the gun in the back of his waistband and put the spare magazine into his shirt pocket.

“Johnny,” Mama D said, “I’m calling 911. Go get your wife and be careful.”

He kissed his son and ran out the door. For a split second, he debated which vehicle to take. The truck would be faster, but they’d hear him approaching, and Johnny might need to sneak up on the bastard. He hopped on the golf cart Nick had arrived in and headed for the house he shared with Lacy.

When he got to the main road, he barely stopped to check for traffic. That’s when he saw the back of Bessie disappearing over the ridge. He couldn't chase the man in a golf cart. Why hadn't he driven his truck? Dumbass. But he had to go see if Lacy was home and if she was hurt.

Outside, there was no sign of Lacy or the man. Only an unfamiliar piece of shit Datsun.

Johnny looked all through the house. In the kitchen, he bent over the sink and splashed cold water on his face, hoping it would clear his head.

A glint of metal caught his eye, and he picked up the coffee cup on the counter. He dumped Lacy's wedding band into his hand and closed his fist around it. He had to get her back from whoever had her, and he had only an inkling of an idea who it might be.

He called Nancy on the way back to Southland and found she was already on her way. Heath's dad, Sheriff Cook, met him at the road, and Johnny hopped in the squad car, ready to flash the blue lights and go after Lacy.

Too late, Johnny realized the sheriff planned to get the license number and search the truck. By the time Johnny got to his own truck, it would be too late to catch them. He fidgeted with nervous energy while he waited for the sheriff to look around. There was nothing Johnny could do to help, and he hated being helpless.

After making sure Nick was okay, Johnny paced the floor of the main house. The sheriff asked him to wait inside, while he and Nancy talked on their phones on the porch.

The sheriff came in the back door. "We have an APB out for Lacy and her car. Heath's guys and mine are splitting patrols and setting up check points. We'll find them." He knelt by the sofa. "Nick, did you hear Lacy call the man by a name?"

Nick shook his head as a tear rolled down his cheek. "He said, 'Come give Stan a kiss'. But Mama Lacy didn't want to. I could tell."

For a moment, Johnny clenched his fists. When he released them, he picked up his son and hugged him close.

"It's him." Nancy came in. "Stanley Riggs, Lacy's ex-boyfriend. He got paroled a week ago. They lived together in North Carolina before he got locked up."

"Oh, God, Nancy," Mama D said. "Is he the one who…"

"Who what?" Johnny asked.

His mama swallowed audibly. "Broke her jaw."

"He broke more than that," Nancy said. "The last time he put her in the hospital, she had eight broken bones. I talked to the victim's advocate who helped put Riggs in jail. She says that based on Lacy's injuries, she's lucky to be alive."

Chapter Twenty-six

Lacy's right eye was swollen to the point her vision had blurred. He'd probably broken her orbital bone…again. The more broken bones she had, the more she learned about human anatomy.

"You got any money in that purse?" he asked. "We need to get a motel room and fast. It's been too long. In fact…" He grabbed a fistful of hair and pulled her head toward his crotch.

"No, Stan." She put her palms on his leg and pushed away.

He lifted his hand to hit her.

"It's not that I don't want to." She raised her arms to block the blow. When it didn't come, she continued, "Ever since my jaw got broken, I can barely eat most days, much less do what you're asking."

Think, Lacy. You've got to give him something, or he'll take everything. She swallowed. "I can use my hands." She cringed away.

"After all this time, all you have to offer is a dry hand job." He snarled.

Her mind raced. "I have lotion in my purse. You won't regret it."

While he undid his pants and slid them down, she looked through her pocket book. She silenced the ringer on her phone and hit the speed dial button for Johnny. After she got the lotion, she set the purse on the floor next to her feet.

Her seatbelt was still latched, but she pulled on the shoulder strap to get some slack. With the lotion on her hands, she swallowed bile and then touched Stan.

He moaned and slid down further in the seat.

She kept one eye on the road and one eye on Stan, waiting for the right moment. Her plan might be foolish enough to work. It might also kill her, but she'd rather die by her own hand than Stan's.

She bit her quivering lip at the thought of hurting Johnny and Nick, but they would be all right. They were strong.

When Stan convulsed and closed his eyes, she let go, disgusted at the thought of his bodily fluids getting on her. Her hands gripped the steering wheel, and she jerked hard to the right. He tried to get control, but because he shot most of his load on the wheel, his slippery grasp was futile.

Bessie flew off the side of the road and flipped upside down. While pressing her back against the seat, Lacy squeezed her eyes shut and prayed. This was way worse than muddin'. She hadn't counted on the steep drop off and Bessie pretending to be a bird who tried to fly…and failed.

They rolled end over end several times, and Lacy let go of the door handle to cover her head as glass flew all around.

She blinked for a long time, and when she opened her eyes, she was disoriented. Her hips and chest hurt, and it took a moment to figure out why. She was hanging upside down, held in place by the seat belt.

She braced one hand on the roof and tried to unhook the belt. It stuck on a good day, and today wasn't a good day. When she braced both arms, she could lift herself enough to take the pressure off, but then she didn't have a free hand to press the release button.

A few more tries and she finally got it. She fell fast, but at the same time tried to roll toward the open window. Glass cut into her back. She crawled out and laid on her side on the ground, her face toward the wreckage.

Bessie was dead.

Then she saw *him*.

***

As soon as Johnny said he had a call coming in from Lacy, the sheriff took his phone. His people used some computer tracking system to locate Lacy, and the first officer on the scene called for medics.

The sheriff told them they hoped it was a rescue, but from the reports at the scene, they needed to be prepared for a recovery mission.

Johnny wouldn't even let his mind go there. He couldn't. He'd promised her she'd never have to be afraid under their roof, and he'd let her down.

His dad had come home from work and drove

them to the hospital. They beat the ambulance.

Johnny held Nick and paced, just like his dad.

"You fellas are wearing down the carpet," Mama D said. "You want me to hold Nick?"

Johnny tilted his chin to see Nick had cried himself to sleep, head on Johnny's shoulder. "I've got him."

Heath came in. "I just left the accident. It was bad. Her car was twenty feet down a ravine."

"Do you have any good news?" Johnny asked, sounding more than a little pissed-off.

"The man was dead on the scene. Lacy was unconscious."

Johnny couldn't help but feel a little relieved that the man who'd caused Lacy so much pain in her life was dead. He just hoped like hell Lacy would live to hear the good news.

An hour later, the rest of the Bakers who lived close by had joined them in the waiting room. His siblings, Maddie, Katie, and Paul, murmured hopeful sentiments, while their kids filled an entire row of seats and behaved like angels.

"Mr. Baker." A man in green scrubs held a swinging door open with his foot.

Three men responded.

He looked at the chart in his hand. "Um, the husband of Lacy Baker."

Johnny stepped forward. "How is she?"

"Fair. We're going to move her to a room soon. I thought you might like to come back and see her through the transition."

Johnny passed Nick to his dad and followed the doctor.

"Thank God," Mama D said.

His family joined in praises and sighs of relief.

When he saw her, Johnny got angry all over again. He wiped his eyes with his fist then pushed her hair back, so he could kiss her forehead.

She opened one eye. The other one was swollen shut. "Nick?"

"He's fine, Little Bit. Just worried about you. We all are. The crew's out in the waiting room."

She attempted a smile, and her already split lower lip split open again and began bleeding. Johnny grabbed a paper towel by the sink and wet one end. He gently dabbed at the blood and applied light pressure to stop the flow.

Her eyes closed again.

"Lacy, I love you." He whispered what his heart had been shouting at him for weeks.

A tear ran from her good eye into her ear. He used the dry part of the paper towel to mop it up.

"Johnny." Her voice sounded small. "Will you stay with me?"

"Until I die," he said.

Because Lacy wasn't up for a lot of visitors, and she didn't want Nick to see her banged up, Johnny told his family to come back the next day. Nick pitched a fit, refusing to budge until he saw Mama Lacy for himself. Johnny relented and made Nick promise not to cry.

Nick made good on his promise. "You got him with a good upper cut. Dad would've been proud." Nick stood on his tiptoes and kissed Lacy's good cheek. "I love you."

"I love you too, baby." Her eyes fluttered

closed as sleep claimed her.

After he sent Nick home with his parents, Johnny took up his vigil by her bed.

During the night, she called out his name. “Lay with me.”

He helped her slide to one side, and he laid next to her, putting his arm over her waist.

She winced.

He lifted his hand. “I’m sorry.”

She pushed the sheet back and lifted her left hip, so she could reach the back of the gown. Helping her pull it up, he wanted to see what hurt.

Johnny gasped when he saw the purple bruising on her abdomen.

“That bad?” she asked.

“Oh, Little Bit.” His eyes were leaking again, so he swiped at them. “This is so not how I wanted to see you naked for the first time.”

She held her side and let out a little gurgle. “Don’t make me laugh. It hurts.”

“Oh, sweetie.” He pulled the gown down and the sheet up. “Is there any place I can touch you that won’t hurt?”

“I think my right boob is in good shape.”

Chapter Twenty-seven

Lacy woke up with Johnny asleep next to her, his deep, relaxed breaths comforting. He was so handsome, and she probably looked like death warmed over. She sure felt like it. Life was not fair.

But he loved her. She'd never had a man be so tender with her.

The door opened, and a nurse came in with breakfast. Lacy didn't get too excited because chewing would be difficult.

Johnny got up, adjusted the bed, and helped her get situated. "Mmmm. Delicious hospital food. I bet it won't taste nearly as good as your cooking." He lifted the cover from the tray.

Grits. She might be able to suck those down, but not unless she doused them with butter and salt first.

Johnny stuck his finger in the grits, and after tasting them, he scrunched up his face. "There's not enough seasoning in the world to fix these." Despite his comment, he began opening salt packets.

The doctor came in before Johnny had her food ready, and since she didn't look forward to the prospect of forcing it down, she welcomed the distraction.

"Good morning, Lacy." The doctor shone a light in her eyes and listened to her heart and lungs. "Sheriff Cook wants to talk to you, but I wanted to check with you first, make sure you're up for it."

She pushed the tray closer to her husband. "Johnny, you can have that."

Johnny grimaced. "Thanks a lot." Then he winked and grinned.

The doctor felt her face and jaw. "I'll order some liquid nutrition."

When the sheriff came in, he patted her foot through the covers. "I'm glad to see you alive, Lacy."

"Me too." She fiddled with the edge of the blanket.

"Riggs is dead."

She'd suspected it when she'd seen him penned under Bessie, but like all evil villains in horror movies, they tended to keep coming until they'd killed their victim. She remembered thinking she'd rest as long as he didn't move then run when she had to.

Lacy looked up and almost said "good" in response to the news but clamped her lips together instead. Even if it was Heath's father, he was the law, and the law normally didn't care much for women with a reputation for going home to their abusers.

Johnny handed her a cup of orange juice with a straw in it.

"I have a question about his condition." Sheriff Cook scratched his chin and looked down. "Was his penis attached prior to the accident?"

Lacy choked on the juice she'd been sipping. It ran down her chin and burned the open cut on her lip. Within two seconds, Johnny was cleaning her up.

He paused, raised one eyebrow, and looked at the sheriff. "The man lost his cock-a-doodle-doo?"

"Ah, yeah. It appeared to have been severed during the crash. Apparently, his Johnson got caught on the steering wheel when he flew through the windshield. Tore it right off."

Johnny put a protective hand over his crotch. "Ouch. Just hearing that is painful."

Lacy sucked on her cheek, until she realized the skin was raw in that spot. "The last time I saw it, it was still attached."

"Saw it?" Johnny asked at the same time the sheriff said, "So his pants were down before the crash?"

Lacy hadn't thought about how this news might affect Johnny, but she wanted him to know. She hoped he'd understand what she'd done was her best hope of getting away.

"Do you want to explain the semen my guys found on the steering wheel?"

Turning away from her, Johnny walked to the window.

She explained that Stan was looking for a motel, so she offered a compromise. She told them about the lotion and calling Johnny and the hand business.

"So he jerked the wheel after you jerked him off." Johnny spoke through clenched teeth. "You thought to call me right before you gave another man a—"

"Johnny," Sheriff Cook cut him off.

Lacy couldn't tell if Johnny was angry with her or the situation. And she didn't correct him on who jerked the wheel.

Johnny let out a breath and rubbed her upper arm. "I'm sorry. I'm glad you called, but I'm glad the sheriff answered. I wouldn't have liked hearing what was happening. I know you only did what you needed to." He pressed his forehead to hers. "You're a survivor. I'm proud of you for fighting."

Heath's dad cleared his throat. "I do have some bad news, Lacy." He looked down and pinched his lips. "It's about your cousin Katrina."

Closing her eyes, Lacy tried to block the emotional blow. She'd wondered how Stan had found out where she was. There was only one person he could ask.

Lacy clawed her chest with her hand, bunching the hospital gown in her fist. If only she could've convinced Trina to move away, make it harder for Stan to find her.

She made herself look at Sheriff Cook. "How did he do it?"

The sheriff furrowed his brow and tilted his head.

"How did he kill her?" she asked again.

"Strangulation. With his bare hands. Her kids

found her when they got home from school."

In a gasp, her breath caught in her throat, and Lacy began to shake. Johnny put his arms around her, hitting sore spots she didn't know she had, but she didn't lean away. The physical pain distracted her from the shattering of her heart.

"Lacy, your back." Johnny lifted his arm.

He'd never want to see her body after this, but she couldn't think about it now.

When she caught her breath, she asked. "Where are the kids?"

"With your mother. Their dad's serving a dime at Eastern Correctional."

"Johnny, I need to get out of here and get them from her." She threw back the covers.

Johnny held her in place. "Wait a second, Little Bit. You're not well enough to leave yet."

"The sheriff in Cherokee County's keeping a close eye on them. You and your mother are the only next of kin they know of."

Moments later, before Lacy could explain the reasons to Johnny, the door opened. Having spoken of the devil, in walked her mom, followed by the kids, who rushed to the bed. Annie let out a loud cry, and Thomas' eyes were red-rimmed.

"It's okay, sweetie. I'm okay. Johnny help her up here with me." She patted the bed.

Johnny lifted Annie, but before he set her down, he said, "Be very careful 'cause she has lots of boo-boos, 'kay?"

Annie crawled beside her, and Lacy put an arm around her. She tried not to wince as Annie buried her head into her shoulder. The poor baby had just lost her mama.

She held out her free hand to Thomas. "Come here."

Thomas walked around the other side of the bed and took her hand.

"You guys know your mama loved you more than anything." Lacy's heart was breaking for her own loss, but even more for the kids.

After a few moments crying and consoling the children, Lacy took a deep breath. "Susan, I'll take them home with me. What arrangements have been made for burial?"

Susan smacked her chewing gum. "The cops got her body for autopsy, so I can't answer that."

"I'll take care of it. Thank you for bringing them here."

"They wouldn't shut up about seeing you—damn little brats. You can keep 'em for all I care." She blew a bubble with her gum and waited until it popped before she continued. "This your husband? I heard you got hitched. Where's your wedding ring? What kind of daughter doesn't invite her own mother to her wedding?"

Johnny took Lacy's left hand, which was wrapped around Annie, and slipped her ring onto her finger.

Ignoring her mother, she smiled at him and squeezed his hand. "Guys, this is Mr. Johnny. He's my husband."

Annie looked over her shoulder at him, and Thomas nodded his head once.

"Have y'all seen Mr. Bobby?" Lacy asked about Trina's boyfriend, a sour taste filling her mouth.

"He cried, Aunt Lacy. And he hugged us and said everything was gonna be all right, but he doesn't know for sure." Annie whimpered.

"Baby, it's gonna be hard for a little while, but we're going to get through it together. Okay?" Lacy smoothed the little girl's hair.

"I can see when I'm not wanted." Her mother turned and left.

The sheriff followed her out, and as soon as the door closed, it opened again. Mr. and Mrs. Baker came in with Nick.

"Hey, Nick. Welcome to the party," Lacy said. "Come meet my cousins. They call me aunt, but we're second cousins. Right, Thomas?"

Thomas nodded.

"Guys, this is Mama D and Big Daddy. They're Johnny's parents."

It may have been the first time she'd called them anything other than Mr. and Mrs. Baker. She hoped the nicknames would put the kids at ease because she was gonna need help with them until she was back on her feet.

Johnny pulled his parents aside to explain things, while she talked to the children. Afterward, Mr. and Mrs. Baker took the kids to get something to eat.

Johnny settled on the side of the bed. "Can I get you anything?"

"I need to see the doctor about getting out of here. I know we need to talk about this." She didn't quite know how to tell him she and her cousins were at his mercy.

"Hey, we'll figure it out. The kids are welcome in our family. You're my wife; we're a team. Like you said, we'll get through this together." He leaned in and pressed a light kiss to her lips.

***

Once Johnny got Lacy home, he propped her up on the king-sized bed, having promised the doctor she would rest. The kids climbed in with her, and after he made popcorn, Johnny snuggled up with them. It was the first time he'd been in their bed. He supposed having three children in various positions removed some of the intimacy. But it was still nice.

They spent the afternoon watching Disney movies and napping. Johnny felt something on his cheek and looked over to see Lacy brushing her knuckles across his skin. He kissed her fingers.

Mama D brought dinner and after the kids had eaten and brushed their teeth, he let them go to sleep in the bed with Lacy. Then, one by one, he carried them to their rooms. He left night-lights on for Annie and Thomas.

When he got back to Lacy's room, he hesitated in the doorway. "I'll stay on the couch."

"I'd rather you slept here with me." She smoothed the spot next to her.

He lay down shoulder to shoulder with her and held her hand. They talked until the wee hours, laughing, crying, and making plans.

"Johnny, I know you married me for Nick, but we're talking about a real future. Is that what you want with me?"

"I do." He hated to ask, but he needed to know.

"Do you love me, Lacy? Do you want to spend a lifetime with a fool like me?"

"You're the fool with my heart." She smiled and touched the center of her chest. "Are you sure about Annie and Thomas?"

"Yes. They're your family, and you're my family. I already spoke to Nancy about us getting guardianship." Once again, his lack of self-confidence made him doubt. "Are you sure you aren't saying you love me because you're afraid I won't help you with them? If you want out, you have the pre-nup. I'll give you whatever you ask for."

Her forehead wrinkled. "Johnny, did you read the pre-nup?"

He shook his head and stared at the ceiling. "I thought it was just boilerplate with your terms. Why?"

"My terms." She chuckled. "I leave with what I brought to Southland, minus Bessie now."

He lifted and turned his head. "Are you serious? You married me without getting anything for it."

"I've already gotten so much. Your love being one of the main things. It also says we have to stay married for at least a year. I hoped you'd be able to love me one day, like I love you."

Damned if he wasn't about to cry. He rolled onto his side and kissed her very softly.

"When I'm better, I think we should…you know…consummate our marriage. Maybe by the New Year." A flirtatious little grin danced on her lips.

"Yeehaw! My wife finally wants to do me," he said in a loud whisper as he popped up onto his knees, jostling her a bit. He leaned closer. "But seriously, Little Bit, there's no rush. When you're fully recovered, we'll talk. And if you want to have another wedding and a honeymoon or anything at all, just say the word."

Epilogue

On New Year's Eve, the entire Baker clan gathered in Gatlinburg, also known as Redneck Vegas. Lacy was mostly recovered from her accident and wearing a white wedding dress for the second time. She walked down the aisle of the crowded little chapel with Thomas on her right and Annie on her left. Nick waited beside his dad at the altar.

As Lacy joined hands with Johnny, she couldn't stop the huge smile, which took over her face. They renewed their vows to each other and their kids.

When Johnny kissed her, he dipped her back, and she put her arms around his neck. She kissed him for all she was worth, which wasn't much in some people's estimation, but to her husband, it was everything. She finally had value to someone. He told her so every day, "more precious than rubies", which was the stone in the heart-shaped pendent he'd given her for Christmas. The new wedding band he slid onto her finger alternated channel set diamonds with rubies. During the ceremony, he said the stones represented love and eternity.

They had a reception in a private room at a nice restaurant, and Johnny hauled her out to the hoots and hollers of the family. He drove them in her huge, new SUV, which he'd also given her for Christmas. A few miles out of town, he stopped at a little cabin, where he carried her over the threshold.

Lacy laughed when she saw the heart-shaped Jacuzzi and mirrored walls in one corner of the bedroom. Thankfully, there were no mirrors on the ceiling.

He set her feet on the floor. "Are you sure you're well enough, Lacy? I don't want to hurt you."

"You won't hurt me, Johnny. You're my gentle giant. Now help me out of this dress." She turned her back to him.

When she was fully undressed, he pulled away to look at her. Her body was marked with scars, and she fidgeted, afraid he wouldn't like what he saw.

"Better?" she asked.

"Beautiful." His eyes simmered with a slow heat.

He laid her down on the bed and took his sweet time kissing every inch of her. She ran her fingertips up his arms, across his shoulders, and down his chest as he positioned himself between her thighs.

He looked into her eyes, and she gave him a welcoming smile as their bodies joined.

Then her eyes rolled back in her head, while Johnny took her to heaven.

***

On a warm day in March, Lacy climbed the ladder to the hayloft for a little afternoon delight. Because the kids were at school and the elder Bakers were away, they figured it was safe.

The rubies she wore symbolized an inextinguishable flame of passion. And that was the God's honest truth. Lacy couldn't get enough good lovin' from her husband.

Johnny laid on the blanket as she stretched out on top of him.

"Okay, I've got one," he said. "We have to decide before the house is finished. Since you're the queen of my heart, what do you think of *Queensland*?"

"I might have a better one." She lifted her head from his chest and grinned. "How 'bout *Loveland?*"

He sat up and rolled her onto her back, kissing his way from her lips to her belly. "Did you hear that, baby? You're gonna grow up at *Loveland.*"

ABOUT THE AUTHOR

Meda White writes sweet, sultry, and southern contemporary and new adult romance. Born with Georgia clay running through her veins, she continues to enjoy the Southern lifestyle with her husband, a very spoiled Collie, and a stray cat who adopted the family. When not writing, you might find her making music, shooting zombie targets, teaching yoga, or explaining the meaning of her unusual first name.

A Note to Readers

Thank you for reading *Fool With My Heart*. I hope you enjoyed Johnny and Lacy's love story. If you feel inclined to leave a review on Goodreads or your online retailer of choice, I'd really appreciate it. I love to hear from you. You can find my contact information on my website MedaWhite.com, and you can also sign up for my New Release Newsletter.

Best wishes for a lifetime of love and laughter. Don't forget to fool around every now and then.

Also Available from Meda White

Play With My Heart

A Southland Romance Book 1

Southern musician and closet geek Liz Baker enjoys her quiet life. While in Los Angeles helping her brother with a house project, the simple life gets complicated when British television actor Ian Clarke walks into the picture.

Ian enjoys his celebrity status in Hollywood and is determined nothing and no one will get in the way of his plans for success on the big screen. He never counted on meeting a woman like Liz, but she's the only one who can help him with a personal problem.

Forced into close quarters where priorities and cultures clash, an intense attraction catches them both by surprise. Secrets, old lovers, and the paparazzi threaten their new dreams and a chance for love could be lost forever.

Dance With My Heart

A Southland Romance Book 2

Traumatized by her past, former police officer Jane Dillon gets a new start in Los Angeles as a bodyguard. If she weren't so good at saving people, she might seek a new career. At least when she moonlights as a dance teacher, no one shoots at her. One impossible-to-please macho boss, one hunk of manly hot action hero, and one oversized Southern family set her on a course she never saw coming.

Former Navy SEAL, Danny Baker, has a lot to deal with between his dad's health, his sister's public breakup, and figuring out how to get rid of a female employee without getting a sexual discrimination suit filed against him. He's always believed it to be his duty to protect women and children, but seeing the beautiful and lethal Jane in action turns his worldview upside down. He'd almost rather go back to the jungle, except the dance floors of L.A. and the woods of Georgia are providing plenty of excitement.

If they can overcome their differences, Danny's family, and Jane's past, they might find that they make the perfect team.

Ride With My Heart

A Southland Romance Book 3

Maddie Baker is back at Southland, picking up the pieces of her broken marriage. When she reconnects with her former rodeo partner, she struggles to remember why they ever lost touch, and why she never revealed her feelings to him.

Georgia State Trooper, Heath Cook, has been avoiding Maddie since she moved home, knowing the crush he's always harbored won't stay hidden for long. If his wasn't the only heart he cared about protecting, it might be different. But his daughter doesn't need to get attached to someone on the rebound.

Renewing their friendship leads to a deeper attraction than either of them experienced as teenagers. With Maddie's jealous ex making a play to win her back, Heath has to decide if he's willing to put his future on the line. And when Maddie's past comes back to haunt her, Heath wants to help, but it may not be in his power. Together, they'll have to see if they can hold on for the roughest ride of their lives.

This contemporary romance contains Southern Gothic elements.

Spring Fling

A Southern College Novella

Kellyn Crenshaw wants to make it to college graduation without becoming another notch on the belt of a fraternity boy. A boy exactly like Pace Samson. Forced into close proximity because their roommates are dating, Kellyn sets out to prove she's resistant to his charms.

Pace never figured himself for a one-woman man until he spends time with Kellyn. She's different, and he can't get her out of his mind. She's also aware of his reputation, and it may keep him from the one girl who makes him want to change his ways.

When Pace and Kellyn fake a fling on Spring Break to help their friends, Kellyn may discover she isn't immune to Pace after all. They'll each have to decide if what's between them is just a fling or if there's a chance their feelings are real.

Fall Rush

A Southern College Novella

Embry Harris is desperate to turn things around her senior year of college. She's determined to make more responsible choices and rid herself of the stigma plaguing her. But because of her job and the hot bartender who goads her into making impulsive decisions, it isn't going to be easy.

Stede Bennett's mission since returning from his overseas tour is to get his degree. The last thing he needs is a spoiled sorority girl distracting him. Being a Marine taught him many things, except how to handle a beautiful woman in constant need of saving.

Protecting Embry from the jerk threatening to ruin her reputation is how Stede begins to lose his heart. Being empowered by Stede's words is how Embry starts losing hers. If the schemer responsible for pushing them together gets his way, they could lose their chance for happiness.

Winter Formal

A Southern College Novella

Life is going according to plan for Sibba Douglas until she gets blackmailed. Her future dream of being a doctor is threatened unless she can help a spoiled fraternity boy do well on the MCAT.

Nash Lincoln knows he needs to settle down and focus on his studies, but academics have taken a back seat to social events, and he's coasting by on little sleep and lots of pills. The distraction of a tutor he's admired from afar isn't helping matters.

Substance abuse leads to tragedy and draws Sibba and Nash closer together. But it may also be the thing that tears them apart.

Christmas Give

A Holiday Novella

Eva Walker returns home to Georgia for the first Christmas since her husband's death. She's missed her family, but is afraid the void left by her husband will make it unbearable.

Between losing his job as an NFL defensive back and losing his wife to the star quarterback, Adam "Mack" Riggs has had a rough year. Looking for a change of pace, he visits an old college friend for Christmas.

The attraction between Eva and Adam is instant, and so is the laughter. Enjoying life again feels so good for both of them. Simple Christmas wishes unite with a shared holiday tradition, putting them on a path toward healing and acceptance. A path that could lead to a future, if only their pasts would remain where they belong.

www.ingramcontent.com/pod-product-compliance
Lightning Source LLC
Chambersburg PA
CBHW061530250926
52052CB00010B/2873